TROUBLE ON CRAZYMAN

TROUBLE ON CRAZYMAN

Noel M. Loomis

First published in Great Britain by Hale
First published in the United States by Lion Books

Published in Large Print 2005 by ISIS Publishing Ltd,
7 Centremead, Osney Mead, Oxford OX2 0ES
United Kingdom
by arrangement with
Golden West Literary Agency

British Library Cataloguing in Publication Data
Loomis, Noel M., 1905–
Trouble on Crazyman. – Large print ed. –
(Sagebrush western series)
1. Western stories
2. Large type books
I. Title
813.5'4 [F]

ISBN 0–7531–7300–X (hb)

Printed and bound in Great Britain by
T. J. International Ltd., Padstow, Cornwall

CHAPTER ONE

The herd of a hundred and eighty dust-laden cows and heifers topped the last high ridge while Blake Summers cracked the end of his lariat at the rumps of half a dozen stragglers.

Red Flynn, two hundred yards ahead, was hazing the cattle along a narrow trail through stunted cedars and huge scattered boulders. He shouted in mock sympathy, "They're tired!"

Blake pulled his roan back into the trail and glanced up. The weather-lines in Blake's face were etched deep with the fine gray dust of the mountains, but he spared only a glance. "So am I," he said, and loped off after a wandering heifer.

They got them all over the hill, watched them spread out in a lumbering run through the deep grass of a dark green Wyoming meadow toward a small creek marked by willows.

Blake said quietly, "Good thing we made it today."

The cows were reaching the creek and wading in. Blake trotted the roan to the right, above the herd. The creek had a gravel bottom, and every marking on the rocks stood out in water as clear as ice — and probably as cold, coming down from the plains on top of the Owl Creek Mountains.

The roan braced itself, its forelegs down in the water, its haunches up on the bank, and skimmed the surface with a questing nose. Blake planted his hands on the saddlehorn and stood up in the stirrups to rest his seat. Blake was medium height, a little on the lean side, with tight lips that made a straight, dusty line in his face, and a sun-browned, wind-toughened skin that made him seem of infinite age without being old.

"Nice little piece of country in here," he said, his far-seeing eyes taking in the little valley from its upper end in the pines, not far above them, to where it disappeared far below among six-hundred-foot straight-up-and-down cliffs of yellow rock. "Good place for a man to settle down."

Red glanced up and then down. "Is this it?"

Blake nodded. "This is it."

Red let his dun mustang have a go at the water. "I still can't see why you had to come back to Wyoming."

Blake said mildly, "I told you that before. We was gettin' ready to be burned out. No snow all winter, up there in Grasshopper Valley. That means no grass this summer. We had to go somewhere. I'm gettin' mighty tired of bein' unsettled," he added, looking far down the valley, "and I want a place to 'light."

Red made a wide sweep with a thick, muscular arm, the gray flannel sleeve caked with trail-dust and sour with the smell of many days' sweat. "You had the whole West to pick from, but you had to come back to Wyoming."

Blake straightened in the stirrups and idly fingered his vest pockets for makin's. "I like Wyoming. Anyway," he added as an afterthought, "there's no warrant over my head."

"There's something worse," Red reminded him. "The Wyoming Stock Growers Association hates your guts. And that means all the big cattlemen."

"That's all gone and forgotten. When Tom Horn was hanged, it cleared the air."

"Then why did you get t' hell out of Albany County and high-tail it for Montana? You never told me that."

Blake frowned and shifted the forty-four in his worn holster. It was a holster that had been in plenty of dry country, for it had begun to crack, and the leather was sloughing away from the cracks. He listened to the roan drink. "There was still plenty of bad blood over the trouble in southern Wyoming."

"You mean you and Tinley woulda fought it out anyway, even after Horn was hanged?"

"Maybe. Tinley never got over it because I branded a couple of mavericks without an inspector present."

"You could as well have had one there."

Blake shook his head. His eyes were bleak. "That maverick law was passed by the Wyoming Stock Growers for the big ranchers."

"A lot of *them* started by running iron on mavericks."

"In those days," said Blake, "they were little and had nothing to lose. Now they're big."

"Did two mavericks mean that much to Tinley?"

"It was what I represented — the homesteader and the end of free range. Tinley was not a forgivin' cuss," he went on, shifting a little as the roan waded deeper into the water. "And he grew up in a hard country, with the law on his hip. After Tom Horn was hanged I knew one of us would have to kill the other one, and I saw no sense stayin'. The hold of the big ranchers was already broken."

"You cleared the way for the little man. You shoulda stayed."

Blake shook his head stubbornly. "A new man on my piece of land was one thing — but me on it was another. It meant a shootout — and Tinley with a family."

Red looked hard at him. "I don't see where Tinley's family made that much difference."

Blake opened his mouth, then closed it. He'd never admitted it in so many words, but sometimes he had wondered if that was the reason.

"You think it'll be different here?" asked Red.

"Mighty different. This is the Wind River Valley and a long way from Laramie. Anyway, the old prejudices are gone. The big ranchers have accepted the homesteaders and the farmers."

"They have?" Red asked sharply.

Blake looked up, his big hat far to the back of his head. "That's what I said."

"Then what's that gent foggin' up the creek for?"

Blake's jaw grew leaner. He turned the roan out of the creek. "You look after the cows." He leaned forward, and the roan began to trot.

There was a dust cloud with a gray horse in it, but Blake did not slow the roan until he drew up to the left of the gray.

A heavy, impatient voice demanded, "What you bringin' them cows over the mountain for?"

Blake was on the side where he could watch the man's gunhand. He was a big, square man with ruddy cheeks and a white mustache, and white hair under a tall hat.

Blake tested him. "Why does a chicken cross the road, mister?" The man's face began to redden. Then Blake said easily, "Who are you asking for?"

"Washakie Cattle Company. I'm foreman of the layout."

"Star Under a Roof brand?"

The square man nodded, his blue eyes probing Blake's. "What's yours?"

"Pronghorn."

"An easy brand to make with a runnin'-iron," the Washakie foreman said bluntly, still watching him.

"Any brand is. Mind tellin' me your name?"

"Cotton Stewart." He paused. "I haven't heard yours."

"I'm Blake Summers."

The white-haired man stared at the cows beginning to spread out over the meadow. Blake couldn't tell what was in his mind, but he found out. "Now that the formalities have been observed" — Stewart's voice rose suddenly — *"get your cattle out of my pasture!"*

Blake studied him. "You make up your mind pretty fast, don't you, Cotton?" he asked.

"I had it made up when I saw that yellow heifer come over the hill."

"You got a right nice mane of white hair," Blake said. "You didn't get that by pickin' fights with strangers."

Cotton Stewart said, "I'm not questioning the ownership of those cows."

Blake hung one leg over the saddlehorn and began to fish for makin's. "I didn't figure you were, Cotton. I bought these critters up at Jackson Lake, and I was told this was the best way to get where I was headed."

"Didn't they tell you this was Washakie land?"

"I don't recall askin'." Blake gave up the search. The makin's were there, but he didn't want to get his hands tied up. This old coot might start slapping leather. "Big outfit you're ramrodding, Cotton."

Stewart nodded grimly. "Eighty sections — and we aim to hold 'em all together."

Blake was far enough down the valley now to see a big ranch-house. Half a dozen hands were standing near saddled horses gathered around the door of the harness-shed.

"Your hands have nothin' to do this time of day but stand around? Must have a big crew."

Stewart's chest swelled but he didn't answer.

Blake said casually, "I filed on a half-section down the valley a piece. I know the upper part of the valley and all of the mountain country in here is Washakie land. I also know that most of it is leased from the government — and that applies to everything on the southwest side of Crazyman Valley." He added softly, "We're drivin' down the other side, Cotton."

Stewart bristled. He said, “You can’t handle that many head on a half-section, Summers.”

“I don’t figger I could, but I bought out a feller.” Blake watched Stewart closely. “A feller who was willing to sell cheap because he’d been choused up by Washakie hands.”

He watched the old man settle back, and he knew he had a tough one. There had been something about Cotton Stewart that Blake had thought at first was a fake, but now he knew better. Maybe Cotton let other men do the actual fighting; maybe they were drawing fighting pay — but there was no yellow in Cotton. Whoever had made him foreman had known what he was doing. Blake kept his eyes on Cotton. “You want to settle this now?”

Cotton’s eyes grew flinty. He didn’t like being backed down, but he turned the gray slowly toward the ranch-house.

Blake went across the creek, wondering why Cotton hadn’t signaled for help; there’d been plenty of it ready.

“Trouble?” Red asked.

Blake looked back; the ranch-house was out of sight behind a ridge of high rock. “No trouble yet,” he said cautiously. “That gent didn’t take kindly to the way we came over the mountains.”

“Gone back for help?”

Blake stood up in the saddle and watched the big man cut around a point of pine trees. “No, I think he’s trying to follow orders, to get used to the idea of us little fellers holing in here and there — but he isn’t making much headway. An oldtimer like him has been on the other side of the fence a long time." He hazed a cow back from the creek. "Keep the stuff on this side. My place is about six or seven miles down."

Red snapped his rope at a lazy heifer. "Nice grass in here — grama grass and muhly grass, knee-high to a tall horse."

Red went on down the creek to keep the herd from crossing. Blake rode behind to catch the tired ones. Red whistled when the Washakie ranch-house came in sight again. "Big outfit. Fifty or sixty hands. Do you expect us two to stand off that many?"

"We aren't alone," said Blake. "The lower part of the valley has been opened to homesteaders since the treaty with the Shoshones and Arapahoes. According to land office records there's eight other homesteads in Crazyman Valley."

"Any way you figure," said Red, "it doesn't sound like more than twenty-five or thirty guns."

"Things are changing," Blake said. "I told you that."

"How?"

"The movement toward small holdings. It's headed that way and nothing can stop it."

"I was born in the Pecos country," said Red, "and there's some things haven't changed since I was born."

"Such as?"

"Men get killed over cattle and grass. I saw my pa shot between the eyes because he believed it was sinful to throw down on a man that wasn't armed." Red looked off down the valley. "The trouble was, pa never allowed for a hideout gun."

Blake watched Red for a moment. Finally he said, "A man has got to make way for a locoed steer once in a while."

Red squared around in his saddle. "Are you allowin' enough?"

Blake slapped the dust out of the roan's mane. "I told you —"

"I heard that — and it suits me fine, but that don't guarantee that we won't be hearin' lead sing before the Washakie people learn about your 'movement'. "

Blake looked back at the big ranch-house. Cotton Stewart had pulled up before the big house and disappeared inside. Blake thought it over. Somebody inside the big ranch-house was getting a report from Stewart and pretty soon a decision would be made.

"Supposing you're right," he said to Red. "You want to take these critters back over the mountains?"

Red looked back upstream. "I got enough dust up there to last me for sixteen years."

CHAPTER TWO

They kept the cows moving down the valley. Blake watched the Star Under a Roof headquarters from the corner of his eye, until, as they passed even with the big ranch-house, he found himself taut. But nothing happened, and five minutes later they were well past the place. Blake drew a deep breath. "It looks like Cotton Stewart is minding his own business," he said. "I tell you, the hanging of Tom Horn did a lot to clear up the atmosphere."

But Red said glumly, "Them big ranchers don't forget."

Blake looked up. "They found out they couldn't scare the little man off with a gunman," he argued.

Red turned to look back at the Washakie ranch-house, but it was out of sight now behind a huge outjutting of yellow rocks, and only the fragrant blue smoke of burning cedar, coming from the kitchen stove and spreading into a thin haze by the time it reached the top of the rock walls, gave any evidence — and even an Indian might have missed that if he hadn't known. To all appearances, now, Crazyman Valley was a place of lush grass and limpid water, where cows grazed peacefully and a woodpecker somewhere below them knocked out a staccato message against a dead tree-trunk.

"Bein' a rancher," Red said, "is a sort of habit. You don't suppose J. J. Tinley —"

Blake said shortly, "Tinley never forgot anything. But we left Tinley in Albany County."

"If there's one like Tinley," Red pointed out, "there's more like Tinley." He watched a cow heading for the hills. "It looks like our herd is gettin' ready to increase," he said.

Blake turned the roan. "I'll go take care of her." He scanned the top of the rocky point, now outlined against the late afternoon sky. "You keep the cattle headed down until you hit a bobwire fence. That's our north line."

He caught up with Red a half hour later. Red looked at the long-legged red-and-white calf across the roan's withers. "You're gettin' a good start," he observed.

Blake grinned. "There'll be more."

Red nodded sidewise. "Are them two fellers company or otherwise?"

Blake studied the two riders waiting at the fence. "Visitors, it looks like," he said finally.

Red said, "I hope they know about the movement."

Blake rode through the spread-out herd, followed by the calf's mother, and up to a gaunt, bony-faced man with long brown mustaches.

"Howdy." Blake dismounted, keeping one hand on the calf. He lifted it off and set it down on its long, spindly legs. Then he looked up with a grin.

But the grin froze on his face. The man was staring openly at Blake's six-shooter, and his bony jaw grew tighter. "Lookin' for trouble?" he asked.

Blake studied him. "No — but not running from it, neither."

The stranger gave it to him straight. "We're peaceful men down here. We ain't aimin' to get mixed up in no range war."

Blake said coldly, "That the way Potter got run off?"

The man hesitated then. "Nice feller, Potter. Peaceful. Nice family too — wife and eight kids."

"But no match for Cotton Stewart."

The stranger looked at Blake again, and unconsciously, as if he couldn't help it, his blue eyes went over Blake's hardware. "That has nothin' to do with it. All us little men talked this over a dozen times. We agreed we weren't big enough to fight the Washakie, so we'd stay peaceful no matter what."

Blake looked at him keenly. "And stay in this valley?"

The gaunt man sounded truculent. "It's our land."

Blake nodded. "I bought out Potter. *He* didn't stay."

"Cotton Stewart never laid a finger on him or his kids," the man insisted. "Potter just — got scared, that's all."

Blake said, "I haven't got eight kids. I don't scare easy."

The man studied him. He seemed to be fighting a battle within himself, but he sighed heavily, and Blake knew the end was the same: this man had convinced himself that by refusing to take up arms he could maintain peace. Finally the man said, "I'm Chester White. This here's my son Docie."

Blake didn't offer to shake hands. He'd wait. "My name is Blake Summers," he said, "and my crew is Red Flynn."

"We're neighbors," said White, "and back in Indiana neighbors aimed to be friendly. But," he warned again, "we ain't gettin' mixed up in no range war."

Blake looked at the rifle in the boot under White's stirrup leather. "Cotton Stewart bothered you?"

White answered slowly, "No. It seemed like he drew a deadline at my fence."

"It's mighty easy to be peaceful," Blake noted, "when it isn't your fence that's cut."

There was again that hesitation. "If trouble ever breaks out on Crazyman," White said, "it'll be bad trouble."

Blake put one booted foot up on the lowest wire next to a post. "If Cotton Stewart could run off Potter, do you reckon he's satisfied to stop at your fence line?"

"He might be."

"Maybe you're right." Blake left the fence. The calf, standing spraddle-legged, was working for its supper with its neck twisted until its head was upside down. The warm milk smell was good in Blake's nostrils. Blake turned back. "Nice to know you, White. Soon as I get a house up I'll invite you in for a visit. By the way" — he rubbed the silk hair on the new calf's back — "what happened to Potter's house?"

White said slowly, "It burned about an hour after he left. They must not of put out their fire."

Blake swung into the saddle. "Be seeing you later," he said.

Chester White and his son mounted and rode away. Blake called to Red, "Get that muley cow away from the rocks. There may be rattlers." They got the cattle bedded down. "Now we'll ride up a little and have a look at where the fence used to be."

"I didn't see even a post hole," said Red sourly. "Maybe Potter crawled in and pulled the holes in after him."

They jogged along. Blake observed, "A man doesn't pull up a bunch of posts and roll up the bobwire and fill in the holes."

Red pulled up the dun mustang. "The fence should of been about here. You said Potter had a section."

"He filed on the bottom half and leased the upper half. I filed on the upper half."

"This looks like an old fence line to me." Red swung his arm across the valley. "See where the grass grows taller in a little bunch every so often?"

Blake sighted. "It's been a fence, all right."

"A horse and a rope could snake a post out of the ground," Red observed, "and then drag the stuff away."

Blake pulled his hat down a little harder. "That means it was done this spring about the time the ground thawed."

They split, and went in opposite directions. Blake found the fence. It had been pulled up into the yellow rocks at the foot of the cliff on the east side. He whistled at Red, and they looked it over together. "We can pull the staples and save the posts," Blake said, "but a man'd never get that wire untangled."

Red got down. "It's been cut," he said. "They couldn't drag it all at once, so they cut it in sections."

Blake got down and looked at the end of wire. "Cut," he repeated. "Cut and drug away." He looked up the valley. The Washakie headquarters was hidden from sight by a bend in the canyon. A few steers were feeding in the valley, and more were beginning to drift down out of the hills toward water. Up the valley somewhere he heard the sudden smothered squawk of a sagehen — almost like that of a chicken — and knew that a coyote had gotten supper.

Blake said, "We'd better scare up something to eat."

A rifle barked at his side and startled him. He heard the click of the lever ejecting the empty case and throwing in a new cartridge before he turned.

Red looked up. "Elk is better than dried beef," he said.

"Sure — but with all this scare talk going around, you might give me warning."

"You know how fast an elk moves," said Red. "Your nerves gettin' on edge?"

They found a way up through ravines, tall, straight pines with orange-colored bark that gave them an ancient, mellow look. Red went to the elk, lying in a clump of sumac.

"Right behind the shoulder blade," said Blake, dismounting. "A nice fat yearling, too."

He threw the reins over a fallen log and drew his skinning knife. They turned the elk on its back, slit the hide from neck to vent and down the inside of each leg. It was half dark by that time, and they didn't hear the man come down through the cedars.

"Nice hunting," he said.

Blake froze for an instant. He moved his elbow far enough to locate the butt of his six-shooter. Then he went back to his work. Both of his hands were bloody and he wasn't in shape for gunplay. This, he realized, the stranger must know. "We got meat," Blake said shortly.

"You don't sound happy about it."

"I don't like being snuck up on," said Blake.

Red began to wipe his fingers with a handful of pine needles. Blake went ahead with his work of laying the skin back.

"What's your name?" asked the voice.

"Summers," Blake said. "Just the opposite of winters."

The stranger remained above them. "My name's Wall — John Wall. Special deputy for the Indian agent here."

Red's hands were dry. Blake flopped the carcass over and went to work on the other side. "Anything we can do for you?"

Wall said, "The top of this divide is the boundary of the Shoshone-Arapaho Indian Reservation. Matter of fact, according to the treaty, Crazyman Creek rises up on the flats inside the reservation."

Blake kept skinning.

"I suppose you know the gover'ment agreed to keep the whites out of the reservation."

Blake looked up. With his eyes partly blinded from the clear brilliance of the sky above the cedars, he could hardly see the man under them. "Never paid attention to it. Never aimed to bust into the reservation."

"A man that trespasses on the reservation," John Wall persisted, "is guilty of a misdemeanor and tried under U.S. law."

Blake stood up and spoke into the half dark. "What the hell are you driving at?"

"You killed that elk on the reservation. I heard the shot on the other side of the ridge. Then you packed it down here to clean it."

Blake demanded, "Are you crazy?"

"You can't get by with poaching on Indian land. Drop that knife on the ground and come up here."

Blake took a deep breath. He dropped the knife; then deliberately squeezed the blood off his fingers. The deputy was still hidden in the shadows under the cedars.

Then Red Flynn spoke, "There's two of us, Wall. Don't try anything."

Blake saw movement in the shadows. He dived head-first over the elk carcass, and rolled. Yellow flame erupted from under the cedars, and he heard the crack of a bullet going overhead. Red's six-shooter exploded in a cone of red fire. The two shots came almost together, and mingled as they rolled down the small canyon, reverberating again and again between the high rock walls.

Blake had Wall's legs before the shots died away. Red helped tie his hands behind him. Blake rolled him over then and struck a match in his face. It was not a pleasant face. The man had a heavy black mustache, and black eyes that gleamed now with rage and impotence.

Blake said to the man on the ground, "Your hand sting a little, sonny?"

The man gritted his teeth in fury.

"You shot the hardware right out of his little fistie," Blake said to Red. "You ruined his gun."

"Sorry," Red said mockingly. "Mighty sorry."

"Who are you?" asked Blake.

"I told you — John Wall, special dep—"

"Who paid you to haze us away from this elk?"

"You violated the I—"

"Would you like to be staked out here all night?"

There was no answer.

"It gets chilly, up so high. Must be about nine thousand feet."

There was no answer.

"Cat's got his tongue," said Red.

"Seems so. Well, have we got any use for him?"

"I'd take elk meat myself," said Red.

They went back downhill. Blake tied up the haunches in the skin and threw them over the roan's withers.

"What'll we do with that special deputy?" asked Red.

"Leave him. He can roll over on his feet."

"He must have a horse around here somewhere."

Blake snorted. "He sure isn't smart enough to steal one." He got into the saddle and called out, "All right, John Wall, or whatever your name is, I'm going to find out who you are and who pays you for dirty work like this."

Wall didn't answer.

Blake began to fish in his vest pockets for makin's as the roan began to work its way down the hill on stiff forelegs. They came out of the ravine into the valley. Blake found the makin's. "Reckon I better tear into Mountain City tomorrow and get the surveyor out here to run our fence line. You can salvage the posts out of that wire. I'll buy a secondhand wagon and a couple of mules, enough wire to string the valley, and some grub. Anything special you want?"

"Yeah," said Red, "a nice blonde squaw."

Blake started to make a cigarette. Then he thought to look up the valley. If they weren't on Washakie land they sure were within gunshot, and a cigarette glowing in the dark made a good target. He flipped away the cigarette and breathed deeply of the night air, now heavy with the scent of pines and cedars. "Sure is a nice country," he observed as the roan jogged along.

"Friendly, too," said Red.

CHAPTER THREE

Early the next morning Blake was up, yawning. "Seems to me the ground is softer than it was up on top of the mountains," he said.

Red grumbled. "These here cows ain't been raised proper. They don't respect a man's boodwar at all." He drew on his boots, folded the horse blanket, and picked up his saddle by the horn.

"Where you goin' with that thing?"

"I —" Red looked around and dropped it. He took his bridle and lariat and struck off for the east side of the canyon.

Blake went down to the creek and washed his face. Down the valley a lark was singing. It was strange, Blake thought, how you heard so few birds singing in a wild country; it wasn't until men came and began to plow up the land and build homes that the birds commenced to sing.

Red returned, riding the dun bareback and leading the roan. "You better start sidelinin' this bronc," he told Blake. "He was away over on Washakie land."

Blake looked at the horse. "Too smart for hobbles, hey?" and added, "Good thing we got up before the Washakie hands."

He had a fire going and two big elk-meat steaks broiling on a rock. A half-gallon peach can was sitting in the fire, and the aroma of coffee began to circulate. Blake split half a piece of pan bread, and they ate in silence. Then Blake got up. He spread the saddle blanket on the roan's back. "Keep the cows off of Washakie land," he said.

"What if Washakie hands come down here?"

Blake smoothed out a wrinkle in the blanket. "Remind them you don't own this outfit." He slid the saddle on easily. "You're just workin' for the Pronghorn brand."

Red looked up from his coffee. "That's supposed to scare 'em?"

Blake reached under the roan's belly with a twig and got the cinch-strap. "Don't be so quick to look for trouble."

"I ain't." Red finished the coffee and rinsed the cup in the creek. "But I'm no fool. It wasn't any accident that John Wall was up there last night. And what about these sodbusters down below? They ain't on our side neither. Chester White told you right out he didn't believe in fightin'."

Blake got in the saddle. "Want me to bring you something?"

"A blonde," said Red.

Red was cinching up the dun. Blake rode off. Half a mile down the creek he rounded a small hill and came out in Chet White's front yard. Chet and his boy Docie were leading a couple of horses into the corral, and Blake waved at them. "Morning, neighbor."

The man seemed to hesitate before he answered: "Morning, Summers."

"Nice day," Blake said as the first full sunlight struck the log cabin.

"Always nice days down here." Chet let his boy take the horses, while he stalked across the hard-packed ground toward Blake. "Did you find that fence?"

Blake nodded. "Drug into the rocks. The wire's too tangled to straighten out. Potter didn't do that, did he?"

Chet shook his head slowly, his eyes on Blake.

"You know a feller named John Wall, a halfbreed Indian maybe, some kind of a deputy on the reservation?"

Chet nodded, his eyes on Blake. "Friend of yours?"

"I doubt it," Blake said dryly. "He had some idea of arrestin' us for shootin' an elk last night."

Chet took a deep breath and seemed relieved when he said, "So that was what I heard last night."

"Yes."

Chet looked at him piercingly. "You musta shot up your meat. I figgered there was at least two rounds fired."

Blake looked down at his saddlehorn. "On the contrary," he said, "it was a nice clean kill."

Chet came closer and looked up into Blake's face. "If you get mixed up with the Indians, Summers, you have to go to the U.S. district court at Lander or Casper. It takes time and money."

Blake looked at the bony-faced man. He noted the anxiety in White's face. Then he asked, "Who's the next man down?"

"That's Luke Leslie. Used to be a big politician at Cheyenne, they say — but I don't know. He keeps to himself. Runs about forty head and does his own work."

"Raising a little corn, too, I see."

"Ten or twelve acres."

"How does it do?"

"Forty bushel to the acre, with irrigation. He built a little earth dam and turns enough water for the corn."

"Who's below him?"

"There's three brothers named Crawford. They're pretty close-mouthed. On the other side of the creek from the Crawfords is Ben Horton. His wife's sick, got a big agy cake and keeps to her bed most of the time. Ben has leased some land in the hills behind him and runs about three hundred head. He's got two hired hands and a Shoshone girl to take care of the cooking."

Blake leaned on the saddlehorn. "Do all these people get along with the Washakie outfit?"

Chet backed away. "They let 'em alone," he said shortly.

"How about the Washakie hands?"

"They go into Mountain City on payday and get likkered up and come back up the road in the middle of the night, but that don't hurt nobody."

"The way you're tellin' it to me, everybody is perfectly happy down here."

Chet considered. "They do what I do, and just what you'll do if you're smart — tend your own business and never mind a little whoopin' and hollerin'."

Blake nodded. "You fellows got families. Also, you aren't next to Washakie land. I am. I don't aim to be pushed around."

"We all came up here to do a little ranchin' — not gunfightin'."

Blake said soberly, "You may not think so, mister, but that's what *I* came to Crazyman for."

Chet White looked him deliberately in the eyes. "I figgered you knew which was the buckin' end of a six-shooter."

Blake turned and moved down the valley. The road wound among rocks and forded the creek occasionally on a hard gravel bed. It seemed well traveled, and Blake guessed the Washakie outfit used it. He thought about Chet White and his talkativeness, which seemed at first not to jibe with his belligerence. But that was maybe understandable. Chet had made up his mind there wouldn't be any trouble, and he was such a hard-headed Yankee he'd keep it that way if he had to fight for it. There was one danger. A man like that, with one idea homesteaded in his mind, was as likely to fight his friends as anybody else. Blake didn't like it . . .

The Crawford brothers built their fences tight. He had to get down to open their gates. They were up, too, for he saw three riders in the hills to the west.

He passed a big two-story cabin and saw a buckskin-clad Indian girl out pumping water. That would be Horton's place then. The Indian girl was about eighteen or nineteen and ripe as a peach in August, and her black eyes were on him almost as soon as he saw her. He turned the roan in toward the pump and got down.

"*Nu'-ah pah'-margh*'," he said in Shoshone. "May I have a drink?"

Those wide black eyes did not leave him. "*O'-se*," she murmured wonderingly, and held a dipper under the pump spout. "*Nau'-ny-hack?*" she asked. "What is your name?"

He had established his point and gotten on her good side, so he answered in English: "I'm Summers, Blake Summers. Bought the old Potter place."

He took a deep drink, emptied the dipper, and handed it back to her, bowl down.

He got back on the horse and rode off without a word. To have indulged in small talk would have lowered him in her eyes — and he might need a friend, any friend, before this was over.

It was kind of an explosive situation, Blake figured, with a sick wife, a healthy Shoshone girl, and a couple of hired hands.

He rode into Mountain City about the middle of the morning. It was a tight little town of maybe fifteen hundred people, with a dusty road running through the middle, a public watering trough in the center of the street, the usual false-front store, a bakery, a pharmacy, bank, hotel, barber shop, pool hall, three saloons and four livery stables, besides the usual general stores and a millinery and dressmaking shop.

He watered the roan in the middle of the street. Then he rode to the Big Horn County Bank and dropped the reins over the hitch-rail. He walked in. The iron wire gratings reached to the ceiling. There were two windows, both open but only one occupied. Blake pulled a folded letter out of the hip pocket of his levis. "I'd like about three hundred dollars on this."

The man at the window read the letter. "Who are you?" he asked.

"Blake Summers."

"You just comin' through or . . ."

"I homesteaded above Chet White in Crazyman Valley."

The banker began to count out gold certificates. "You want all this in cash, I take it."

"Yes."

"Two eighty, three hundred." He picked up the stack of bills and began to count them again. At one hundred he stopped and stared at Blake. "I'm not interested, Mr. Summers, in the question of the big man against the little man. We'll always have big cattlemen because ranching is essentially a big business. I think we'll always have little ranchers too — but," he added softly, "a man with eight children had no business homesteading so close to the Washakie range."

Blake took the money, put it in his shirt pocket, and buttoned the pocket. "I have no children, Mr. —"

"Miller," said the banker. "Perry Miller." He extended his hand through the window, and Blake shook it.

"Like I said, I have no children, and I sure hope the Washakie people don't take offense at me because of it. I came to stay."

Miller nodded as he looked Blake over. "If I were you," he said, "I'd roll up that gun-belt and carry it under my arm. This isn't Montana. There's a city ordinance."

Blake's eyes narrowed. He looked at the banker. Then he unbuckled the heavy belt and wrapped it with the pistol inside. "How much do I owe you for cashing this?"

"Not a thing, Summers. Glad to give you a lift."

Blake went to the hardware store. The wooden floor was old and shaky, and Blake's spur chains jingled as he walked across the boards. "Got any bobwire?"

The hardware man looked at him over his glasses. "How much do you need?"

"Ten spools."

"When do you want 'em?"

"Tomorrow noon."

"They'll be ready. What's the name?"

"Summers."

"Live around here, Mr. Summers?"

"Up Crazyman Creek."

There was a pause. "Is this cash, Mr. Summers?"

"It's cash," Blake said crisply.

"Homesteaders don't seem too permanent up that way."

"Neither does fence. Where can I buy a team of mules and a second-hand wagon?"

"Carthy's Livery, past the watering trough."

"Thanks."

Carthy was a one-eyed man who had a light wagon for fifteen dollars and a team of mules for fifty dollars apiece. Blake said, "I'll pick them up tomorrow morning. Here's forty dollars to hold them."

"Good enough. What are you goin' to use for harness?"

Blake was buttoning his shirt pocket. "Good thing you mentioned it. I'd look funny skinning these mules without harness."

"I've got a used set you can have for five dollars. A better set for twenty."

Blake looked them over. "I'll take the twenty-dollar set."

He rode out of the sour horse smell of the stable into the bright sunlight. He stopped at the Land Office to report that he had occupied the homestead. The U.S. commissioner was a tall, sandy-haired man by name of Conway.

"You say you brought some cows over the mountains?"

"Yes."

"I don't know whether you are aware of this, Mr. Summers, but the Indian agency in Lander is a mighty good market for beef. The Shoshones and Arapahoes have to eat, and the government has a treaty under which we have agreed to furnish so much beef per day per Indian."

"There's plenty of cattle in this country, isn't there?"

"There is plenty — but most of the big ranchers seem to think the Indians ought to be starved out of existence. Some of them would rather ship to Omaha for eight cents a pound than sell here in Mountain City for nine cents."

"I always figured," Blake said, "that an Indian has to eat like anybody else."

Conway drew back. "Thought I'd mention it. We have just closed a two-year contract with the Washakie outfit, but I'm not sure they can handle it."

"Then how did they get it?" Blake asked bluntly.

"Because they were the only sizable outfit in the country that would take it on. By the time your calves get big enough to butcher, we'll likely be able to use them."

"Count me in," said Blake. He asked curiously, "Why can't the Washakie outfit deliver plenty of beef?"

"Their leased land is not very good grazing land. Down in the valley, five acres will fatten a steer, but up where they are, it takes fifteen or twenty acres."

"I suppose the government would like to keep the contract in one piece if it could."

"We would, but there's still more at stake. There are bigger contracts coming up over in the Blake Hills, to feed the Sioux. Figure it out for yourself. We pay a cent above the market, and no shipping expense."

"When my calves get eating size," said Blake, "you'll hear from me." He picked up his rolled gun-belt from the desk. "Where can I find a surveyor?"

Conway said slowly, "Right down the street, across the bank. There's no sign."

"Thanks." He loop-hitched the roan in front of a general store and went down the street. The door needed a coat of paint, he thought, as he pushed it and went in.

CHAPTER FOUR

Blake hesitated for an instant as he faced a rolltop desk piled with books and papers, and an unpainted back door. Four surveyor's rods, marked off in white with black figures, stood in a corner. A drafting table was set up against the one window — a large table with a slanted top and a number of big sheets of paper held on with pins stuck slantwise in the upper corners. On the floor under the table was a surveyor's transit, and in a chair before the table, with a steel pen poised carefully in her hand as she turned, was a young woman.

She was slender in certain places but solidly filled out in others. She was dark-haired and wore glasses. Her skin had a mellowed quality as if she had done considerable riding; her lips were red, and her upper eyelids were quite full. When Blake got over his astonishment, he realized that he had checked her over as carefully as he might have a young heifer.

She looked steadily at him without speaking, but her eyes were taking him in, though he had no way of knowing what her reaction was — and well she might be reserved, he thought, in a frontier town like this.

Blake took off his hat. "I'm looking for the surveyor, ma'am."

She was wearing a long, dark brown skirt, and a white shirt-waist with a high, tight collar. She was quite self-possessed, and he began to see that she was not as much of a child as he had thought. She had a maturity about her that usually came only to older women, and he knew instinctively that she had had it all her life, but she also had a freshness, a vigor and interest, that most likely would be with her always.

"All right."

"Are you the surveyor's wife, ma'am?"

"So far," she said evenly, "I'm nobody's wife. My father was the surveyor in old Fremont County; my mother died when I was young, and so I was with father quite a bit. He sent me East to college, but after a couple of years I came back home and he made a surveyor of me. When he died, I kept it up. I make a living, and it is work I like — being outside a good deal, riding over the mountains. Who are you?"

"Blake Summers."

"All right, Mr. Summers. I believe you said you want a surveyor. Are you satisfied to deal with me?"

He smiled. "More than satisfied, ma'am. I wish all surveyors were as pretty as you."

"About the surveying, Mr. Summers," she said patiently.

He took a deep breath. She was a provocative little wench to look so decent — and provocativeness in a rough country was not at all unwelcome, for unfortunately most women were either strait-laced and scared to smile at a man, or they hung around a saloon, thickly painted to hide their age and their weariness, and always ready with a hard smile if there was money in it. Getting tied up with the first kind was like buying a rooster in a tow-sack; some men were lucky and some weren't; there was no way of telling ahead of time. And associating with the second kind always made him feel that he needed a bath.

Blake laid his rolled gun-belt on a small table that held a kerosene lamp. "I want you to run my fence line across Crazyman Valley at the upper end of what used to be Potter's leased pasture."

She studied him without showing what she thought. "I ought to make you a special price," she said. "I've run that line so often I could do it in the dark."

"Run a good one this time," he suggested. "I want it to stick."

"I'll ride out day after tomorrow, in the morning. If you can help me with the rods, it won't take very long."

"I'll sure help, ma'am —"

The front door banged open. Blake turned to face John Wall.

The deputy, coming in out of the blinding glare of the sun, did not notice Blake at first. "Afternoon, Miss Blendick."

The Big Horn County surveyor said, "Come in, John."

"I — pardon me. You got comp'ny." John Wall squinted. "Summers!" His voice was suddenly hard.

Blake watched the man as he said, "I'm Summers. Just the opposite of winters, like I told you last night."

"I been lookin' for you."

Blake's glance took in the man's gun-belt and the pistol in a holster. "I thought we settled that elk business," Blake said stiffly.

"It ain't that," Wall said. "I heard you was wearin' a gun here in town."

"Who told you that?"

"It doesn't make any difference who told me."

Blake lifted his heels off the floor. "It does to me," he said, and noticed Miss Blendick moving to one side.

Wall advanced a step. "You got a gun on you?"

Blake demanded, "What difference does it make? This isn't the Shoshone reservation."

"I'm marshal of Mountain City," said Wall. He moved toward Blake.

Blake said harshly, "Don't put your hands on me, Wall, unless you want to fight."

Wall hesitated. He made a movement toward his pistol. Blake tensed. Then Wall's arm straightened out. "That your gun in the roll there?"

"It is."

"I'll just take it along with me."

He reached for it. Blake brought the edge of his hand down hard on the man's biceps. Wall grunted, jerked his arm back and dug for his pistol.

Blake didn't reach for his gun roll. He didn't have time. He closed with Wall and caught his wrist. But Wall was as strong as a bull elk. He lifted Blake off his feet with his arms.

Blake swung both hard-toed boots at the man's knee caps. Wall dropped him and jerked at his wrist, but Blake closed again and turned Wall's gun arm behind his back. He pushed up in a hammer-lock and swung around to the side to finish it. But Wall had his pistol with his left hand. Blake dropped the man's right arm and knocked the gun hand down. A bullet ploughed into the floor, and the small office filled with black smoke and acrid fumes.

Blake caught the pistol with both hands and twisted it away. He tossed it toward Miss Blendick and stepped back to slug Wall on the chin. Wall buckled in the middle and started to sag.

Then the back door crashed open and a gravelly voice filled the room: "What's going on here?"

Blake froze. He'd know that voice anywhere on earth. That was the man who had testified against him for branding two mavericks in a technical violation of the law; that was the man who had hated him for homesteading on a nice piece of land with some running water; that was the man to protect whose children Blake Summers had left Albany County. J. J. Tinley.

Blake came to a careful stop. "Hello, J.J.," he said slowly.

Tinley's eyes didn't widen, and Blake knew then that Tinley had known all about him, undoubtedly had watched his movements from the time he had hit town, and had sent John Wall to corner him in Miss Blendick's office.

"Please forgive me, Roberta. I heard a shot —"

She said coolly, almost with amusement, "You needn't worry about me, Jefferson."

Blake's jaw hardened. He drawled at Tinley, "Last time I saw you, you was scratchin' to feed three children, with another one on the way."

Tinley whitened, and Blake felt, rather than saw, Miss Blendick glance at him. "Why, Jeff," she said, "I never knew you had a family."

"They're all grown," Tinley said harshly. "My wife's dead."

"They couldn't all grow up in six years," Blake said.

Tinley's eyes narrowed. "I heard this man was wearing a gun," he said, looking at Miss Blendick through the smoke.

"I'm not," said Blake. "But *you* are."

Tinley stared at him. "I'm mayor of this town," he said.

"Mayor?" Blake tried hard to add it up.

"Is that your gun-belt?"

"It is," said Blake, holding the man's eyes, and wondering, as he had done many times before, what it was that gave them a hunted look.

"I'll just take it along," said Tinley, "before you get into further trouble." He moved toward it.

"No you won't," Blake said firmly. "I'm a peaceable citizen, minding my own business."

"Then obviously you have no need for a weapon," said Tinley.

But Blake held him with his eyes. "Not all the citizens of Big Horn County are as peaceable as I am. You'll have to kill me to disarm me."

Tinley's face was whitening again, in two spots just below the temples. He looked at Miss Blendick and then at Blake. He reached for the rolled belt.

Tinley was holding his own pistol in his right hand and reaching across his body with his left. Blake stepped in fast, with his arms down, and slammed into Tinley's body with his own. Tinley stumbled back. He brought up the pistol, but Blake pushed it away and swung for Tinley's jaw.

He checked the swing in mid-air, for he felt a pistol hard in his back. He let his arm drop slowly. Tinley smiled a thin smile. He turned the pistol over and brought it down on top of Blake's head.

The front sight tore a chunk out of Blake's scalp. Roberta Blendick gasped. Blake gritted his teeth, but the gun was still hard in his back. Tinley swung again. Blood poured over Blake's left eye and blinded it. Tinley's face was red now, choleric with the rage he was working out in this gunwhipping. He kept swinging, up and down, his arm rising and falling, the front sight cutting great furrows in Blake's scalp, until he was drenched with blood and numb to pain.

He stood there. He was still standing there when John Wall took the pistol muzzle out of his back. He was still able to hear Tinley's animal grunt of satisfaction as his hot breath whistled in and out. He heard Tinley say, "That ought to hold him for a couple of days." Then he sank down slowly.

He was stretched out on the floor when he came to. He knew he hadn't been out long, for Roberta Blendick was calling to somebody through the front door, “Get Doctor Adams!”

She came back to Blake. He opened his eyes and saw her shaking her head.

“Don’t be upset,” he said. “It isn’t near as bad as it looks.”

Her voice wasn’t too steady. “You’d say that if you were dying.”

“I’m not dying,” he assured her.

She touched his arm. “Can you hear what I’m saying?”

Blake licked blood off his upper lip, “Yes.”

“I saved your pistol for you. I told him it would look better for him.”

“Thanks.”

With her help he got up to a sitting position. His head whirled for a moment. He looked into her face, very close to his.

She kept her hand on his back. “Are you going through with that fence line?”

“Sure. Just because Tinley is mayor of Mountain City —”

“Mr. Tinley is more than that, Blake. He’s president of the Washakie Cattle Company just above you.”

Blake stared. “Washakie?”

She nodded.

“Well, it makes no difference,” he said at last.

She took a deep breath. “I’ll be there day after tomorrow, then.”

“I’ll be waiting for you, ma’am.” He looked down at the blood on his vest. He started to hunt for makin’s, but the tobacco sack was soaked. He tossed it away and got up unsteadily.

"They took your cartridges," she said, "but they're forty-fours and I've got some in the desk there — I shoot a Winchester — if you promise not to go hunting for him."

Blake smiled. "You're mighty kind to a mav'rick, ma'am." He dropped a dozen cartridges in his other shirt pocket. "I'll pay you for these when we settle up day after tomorrow, ma'am. What I don't understand is why you're so anxious to see me armed."

Her mouth dropped open for an instant. She avoided his eyes. Then she said slowly, "I liked Mr. Tinley. I didn't know he could be so brutal."

Blake said grimly, "You ain't seen nothin', ma'am. Wait till I get Tinley down to *his* hole-card."

She shuddered. "I'm sure you would not gunwhip a man while somebody else holds a pistol at his back."

"I'm sure you're right, ma'am."

The door opened and a short man with a full black beard came in and set a black case on the table by the kerosene lamp. "Another gunwhipping, eh?"

He looked at Blake's scalp. "You're a mess, young man. What did you do to deserve anything like this?"

"That," Blake said, "depends on the viewpoint."

The doctor nodded. "You'd better come over to my office and let me sew up your scalp. The shape you're in now, you'd be a disappointment to a Piegan. Can you walk?"

"Sure." Blake tucked his gun-belt under his arm. "Thanks, Miss Blendick. Thanks for everything."

He saw her white face in the doorway, and when she didn't answer he realized that she was about to faint. "Wait a minute, doc," he said.

She slowly curled up on the floor. "You better give her some smellin' salts," said Blake. "I'm in no hurry."

"Roberta is a very resourceful woman," the doctor commented, raising her shoulders and holding a small bottle under her nose.

"She sure is," said Blake, "but she'd play hell holding a job in a slaughter house."

CHAPTER FIVE

J. J. Tinley was cleaning the skin and caked blood out of his gunsight.

"You worked him over right," John Wall said after a silence.

Tinley looked through the second-story window at the watering trough below. He pointedly avoided seeing Wall. "It was about time somebody did," he said sarcastically. "*You* weren't getting anywhere with him."

"I was doin' what you told me to do."

Tinley snorted. "A man like Summers has got to be taken care of permanently. That Summers is a bad hombre."

"But J.J., I never had no excuse for shooting him down."

Tinley looked up, disgust on his hard face. "If you weren't so damned careful and afraid you'd hurt somebody, it'd all be over now."

Wall thought it over. "Look here, J.J., you didn't tell me you wanted Summers killed."

"I didn't think it would be necessary."

Wall frowned again. Abruptly he stared at Tinley.

"Everybody knows I'm fast with a gun — and everybody knows I work for you. When I throw down on a man, I've got to be in the clear."

"What do you think I'm payin' you a hundred a month for — fixin' windmills?"

Wall stood up. He wasn't as tall as Tinley, for he had no neck to speak of, but he was big-boned and considerably heavier.

Tinley finished wiping the blood off his sight while he gave Wall plenty of time to figure it out.

"I tell you," said Wall, "I just can't go around throwing down on a man. Everybody knows how fast I am, and —"

Tinley spun on him. "Fast, hell! Blake Summers can start with both hands in a bucket of tar and beat you to the draw every time." He hesitated an instant. He hadn't meant to say that.

But Wall didn't take the bait. He was undoubtedly turning over, in his slow mind, what Tinley had said about Blake's speed with a gun.

"J.J.," he said, "you never told me Summers was that good."

"I didn't want to scare you," said Tinley, watching Summers follow the doctor into his office across the street. Tinley made a mental note; the next time he beat up Summers, the man wouldn't walk to the doctor's office; he'd make sure of that.

Wall said slowly, "You might of got me killed, J.J."

"Naw, he isn't that good."

But Wall persisted. "Then you figgered I'd kill him."

"Well?" Tinley was becoming impatient.

"All you told me was to take his gun away — and that's all I tried to do."

Tinley dropped his six-shooter in its holster. "Never mind," he said. "I think I got more fun out of gunwhipping him anyway."

"What do you want me to do now, J.J.?"

"You better stay out of his way as long as he's in town. He'll be in a bad humor when he gets sewed up." He tossed Wall a silver dollar. "Here, get a couple of quick ones and head for the reservation till this cools over."

"How about if I find him up above your place?"

"Even you ought to be able to figure that out," Tinley said sarcastically. "If you catch him on reservation land, arrest him — and don't stand and palaver the way you did last night. You know by now that Summers is poison."

Wall put the dollar in his pocket. "All right, J.J."

Wall stopped in the saloon and had two drinks. That left him sixty cents, which he put away slowly and methodically. He did everything slowly — everything but draw and fire a pistol. When he was up against another man who might kill him, his brain was always clear and his arm was lightning fast. He knew one thing: he had to point his pistol in the direction of the other man's wishbone and he had to do it first. He had become very good at that — good enough so most men in Big Horn County walked around him. It made him feel good to think about that, but he was puzzled and confused because Tinley had not warned him about

Summers. He considered that as he pocketed the sixty cents. Then slowly he lifted the heavy little glass and drank.

He left the saloon by the back door, found his star-faced bay at the hitch-rail in the rear, and set off toward Crazyman Valley.

It was well after dark when he drew up to the big Horton house. He sat the bay for a moment, trying to see inside, but the window where he usually looked had a curtain pulled across it, and he knew Mrs. Horton had been up and around that evening. He walked the bay around to the back and stopped where he wouldn't be in the light when the back door opened. Then he made an odd sound in his throat, like a woodpecker drilling on a hard-resined pine tree.

Presently the back door opened, and Soft Hands stood silhouetted by the kerosene lamplight. John Wall took a deep breath. Soft Hands was shaped like the surveyor girl in Mountain City, but not as fragile; she'd not only be good on a buffalo robe but strong enough to husk corn and dig post-holes.

She stood framed for a moment. Then she stepped down, and her soft voice came to him in the darkness: "Johnny!"

He was down, holding the bay's reins in one hand. She came up to him quietly on her moccasins. Her eyes were at the level of his chin. He put out big hands to touch her ripe softness. He kissed her hard, and she stood on tiptoe and kissed him back.

His breathing was harsh when he said, "When are you coming to live with me?"

She did not move back away from him, but stayed in his arms, with her hands on his chest, her fingers picking playfully at his shirt button. "I do not know, Mr. Gun Shooter."

"Why do you call me that always?"

"The white men call you that. They say you are Mr. Washakie's Gun Shooter."

"It don't make any difference what they say." His voice was fierce. "When are you coming with me?"

She dallied. "I do not know. You ask the chief."

"You said that before, and when I asked him you said we were modern, I had to ask you."

"I not know," she said naïvely, "if you are modern. Your mother is Arapaho, your father is white. Is that not so?"

"That is so."

She picked at the button. "Then I now know what you are. I not decide to get married Indian way or white way."

"What's the difference?"

"Is difference to me. If I am marry the white man's way, you cannot divorce me by walking out of house."

Wall was perplexed. "You said once you wanted to live in a teepee, the Indian way."

"Maybe I have change my mind. White man's house is warm, plenty room for kids."

"You lived in white houses and got big ideas," Wall said.

"Oh, now, Johnny . . ."

He took the kiss. Then he backed off. "You're like that surveyor woman in Mountain City. She should of been married ten years ago and raised a lot of kids by now."

"Does a woman have to start raising kids right away?"

For a moment his failure to understand her supplanted his desire for her. He held her at arm's length. "Is it wrong — to raise kids?"

Her soft arms were around his neck again. "Not wrong — but there are other things too."

Now he was utterly confused. "I don't understand you, Soft Hands. You change every day."

"I no change," she insisted.

John Wall growled, "Is somebody else slippin' down here?"

"Who would dare?" she asked.

John Wall didn't know. There was only one man in Big Horn County who wasn't afraid of him. That was Blake Summers, and he hadn't been in Crazyman but one night. Wall kissed her violently. Then he climbed into the saddle and loped away into the blackness of the deeper valley.

CHAPTER SIX

The next morning in Mountain City, Tinley stopped in at the saloon on his way to breakfast. He spun a silver dollar on the mahogany, and the bartender set out a bottle of Madison Club Whisky. "See John Wall around here yesterday afternoon?" he asked as he killed the first one and poured a second.

The bartender nodded. "He was in. Had a couple of quick ones and went out the back door."

Tinley pushed the change back. "Hear anything about any trouble in town yesterday?"

"Some," the man said cautiously. "Hear there was a gent sewed up in Doc's office last night."

Tinley poured another. "Where's the gent now?"

"He was in last night with his head all wrapped up. Got roarin' drunk and had a fight with two gents from up on Cottonwood Creek."

Tinley looked up quickly. "Are you spoofing?"

"Not me."

Tinley threw out another dollar. "Give me a fistful of Doña Josefas," he said. "You're sure it was the same man?"

The bartender held out a cigar box. "That's the way it was told to me."

"What were they fightin' over?"

The bartender raised his eyebrows and leaned over. "One of these gents made a remark about the lady surveyor, and this gent — Summers, somebody said his name was — took exception to it. He wasn't wearin' a gun, so they sailed into him. They looked pretty good for a minute or two, but when he got the range he laid 'em out like a couple of gut-shot antelope."

"What happened to this gent afterwards?"

"Carthy dropped in this morning and said Summers went up to his place to sleep it off in a pile of straw."

"Why didn't Carthy throw him out?"

"Summers had just bought a wagon and team from Carthy."

Tinley left the saloon with four drinks under his belt — and still stone sober. Damn that Summers! He'd always been like that. You couldn't kill him with a ton of brick. The gunwhipping he'd had yesterday should of sent him out of town on the next train.

The fool didn't have sense enough to know when he was licked.

Tinley turned into the hotel for breakfast. The smell of eggs and ham was good to his nostrils. He made his way to a small oilcloth-covered table and sat down with his hat on. A pudgy man in a derby, wearing nose glasses, looked up from his paper. "Morning, J.J."

"Morning, Floyd. How's the legal business?"

"They're opening up eight more sections of land on Poison Mountain, according to the paper. That means sixteen homesteaders — final proofs and all."

Tinley scowled. "More land for the sodbusters. Who's going to raise beef for the country to eat?"

"Beef'll be raised," said Floyd Rawson. He put aside his paper as the waiter came in with a big white platter and a mug of steaming coffee.

"What'll you have, Mr. Tinley?"

"The same."

Tinley picked up the paper.

"You might as well not fight it, J.J. There's going to be more people in here every year. The population of this country is growing all the time. They've got to go somewhere."

Tinley leaned over. "You like being counsel for Mountain City, don't you?"

The pudgy man stopped in the middle of a bite, his eyes big under his derby hat. "Certainly I like it."

"Maybe you're gettin' ready to change sides," Tinley said.

Rawson stopped again, his fork poised. "You know better'n that, J.J. I never —"

"Shut up!" said Tinley. "Here he comes now."

Rawson gulped down his bite and looked around. "Who? The gent with his head wrapped up?"

Tinley nodded.

"Who's he?" asked Rawson.

"Don't you ever stir out of that stinking office of yours?"

Rawson looked hurt.

"This owlhoot ranny had a disgraceful fight in the saloon last night with a couple of peaceful cowboys from up north."

"Your saloon?"
"Yes."
"We'll slap a peace bond on him! We'll —"
"He's poison. You'll leave him alone till I say."
Rawson finished his ham, watching Summers sit down at the counter. "For a gent that got so bad beat up, he looks pretty spry this morning."
Tinley did not enlighten him. At about that time Summers saw him. He got up at once and came over. "Morning, J.J.," he said. "I see you aren't carrying any hardware this morning."
"I never carry it," Tinley said coldly, "unless there is trouble."
"I'll let you in on something, J.J. There's liable to be trouble any time from now on. You better go loaded."
Tinley started up. The dining room was suddenly quiet. But Summers put a lean hand on his shoulder and pushed him back down in his chair. Floyd Rawson jumped up and back, his coffee untouched.
Summers said savagely, "I'm always in a bad humor after a gunwhipping. Come on up and we'll finish it now!"
Tinley looked at him. He saw the knots in Summers' jaws. He sat quietly where he was and said, "I can't hit a sick man," and reached for the glass of water.
"You can't hit a *man* —"
Tinley hurled the glass into his face and arose with it. He hit Summers three times before Summers got the water out of his eyes. By that time Summers was groggy. Tinley hit him three more times, and Summers stumbled over a spittoon and fell backward.

Tinley stood over him for an instant, then straightened up and walked out.

"Your breakfast is ready, J.J."

"I lost my appetite," Tinley said haughtily. "I never could eat in a barnyard."

He went to the saloon and had two more drinks, with one eye on the door. "You got my gun under the backbar there?"

"Where I always keep it."

"Be sure it's handy."

The two drinks didn't help him much. He was shaking inside, and nobody knew better than he. There'd be an all-out fight between him and Summers sooner or later.

Now that they were on the road to a showdown, Tinley almost wished he had tried to compromise and stop the homesteading at Summers' south line. But he thought that over on another drink, and found it was no good. He had drawn the line at Chet White's, and there it would have to be held. If he let Summers take another section, somebody else would take another, and pretty soon the whole valley would be full of sodbusters. The line had been drawn and it was up to him to hold it. And that hadn't ought to be so hard, with forty gunfighting hands against Summers and whatever help the man could stir up.

There was, as Tinley saw it, only one possibility: Summers might recruit the sodbusters to make a fight of it. He might — you never knew what Summers might do. Maybe there were other ways to put pressure on the man.

He went up to the land commissioner's office and found Conway wiping the dust off the window.

"We sure ought to have a street sprinkler in Mountain City," said the sandy-haired commissioner.

"We'll have it," Tinley said easily. "These things take time — *and* money."

Conway laid the damp rag on the window sill. "How's your beef coming?"

"Good enough," said Tinley.

"I was down at Otto day before yesterday and ran into the Indian agent from Lander. He said that last bunch of stuff wasn't so good."

Tinley reared back in his chair. "As good as anything in the country this summer!"

"That isn't what counts. The government guaranteed by treaty to feed these Indians, and this is one time we're going to do it. There'll be no more stampeding the beef issue as there was in New Mexico a few years back."

"I don't know why you're talking to me. I'm making delivery according to the contract."

"Except for condition," Conway told him. "They think in Lander that you cut out the poorest stuff you could find."

"It isn't easy to raise good beef any more since they opened up Crazyman Valley to the sodbusters. That's the best grazing land in the country. I used to send my steers down there for fattening; the way it is now, I've got no place to fatten them."

Conway was digging a pipe out of a desk drawer. "You've got lots of land up there."

"That mountain land is no good without water. When there's plenty of snow we have plenty of grass, but when it's dry we don't have any."

Conway filled his pipe. "It's true enough you've got to have water up in the mountains if you're going to be sure of anything. The Shoshones and Arapahoes found that out." He held a match over the bowl of the pipe and sucked in the flame. "The Shoshones have been trying to irrigate for a good many years, but they don't know anything about it and they haven't got enough equipment to do more than raise a garden."

Tinley sat up. "The Indians using water to irrigate?"

Conway looked at him. "Sure. The old treaty provided they should have water to raise crops — say, there's an idea!" He struck the desk with his hand. "They've never made good use of it, as I said, and there's a suit in court now to cancel their water rights as of 1868 on the ground that it was made without the consent of the state of Wyoming."

Tinley felt excitement begin to rise in him.

"If those Indian rights are cancelled," Conway said, "then there will be a lot of footage available on upper Crazyman."

"A man could build a damp up there and irrigate his own valley," said Tinley.

Conway nodded over his pipe. "The only thing is, it's too indefinite. That case may not be decided for years. How about over on Gunsmoke Creek, where Miss Blendick has her homestead? There's unclaimed land over there."

"It isn't big enough for me," said Tinley.

"Well, look, I have no personal interest in this one way or another, except to see that the Indians don't go hungry, but why not buy out the men on Crazyman? They've all been up there long enough to have rights."

"Who'd sell?"

"I'd start with old man Leslie. His arthritis is pretty bad and I don't think he can stand another winter."

"It's worth looking into."

"Then there's the new man, Summers. I understand he has to build over from scratch, and maybe he'd sell out if you offered him a good price."

"Summers is a tough nut, I hear."

"Well, there are others. You might have to pay a little over the market to buy up the valley, but it would be worth it. You're bottled up the way it is now."

"I'm —"

"Look. If you bought out everybody in the valley, you could put beef-raising back on a big scale. And that's what we need. I've encouraged the small ranchers in the valley all along, but from our standpoint we'd really rather see it in the hands of one owner. It makes dealing easier, the way I see it. And we can keep the redskins fed without so much finagling. That is saying nothing of the big beef contracts in the Black Hills. Any man who shows the government that he can and will produce beef is going to have a sweet market here in the next few years."

"Maybe," said Tinley, "you've got a good idea. Maybe I *could* buy them out." He went out onto the wooden sidewalk. Blake Summers would never sell, but if he could buy up everybody else, he'd make things so hot for Summers that he'd be glad to sell.

CHAPTER SEVEN

Tinley went out feeling better. He went back to the hotel. The dining room was empty, but with a good many obsequious *yes sir's* the cook fired up the wood stove again and prepared breakfast. Tinley took his time, in the half-dark of the dining room. Outside, the sun was blindingly bright, and the light brown dirt reflected it like a mirror.

This was the best time of the day for Tinley. Outside, the sun was heating up the world; dust was rising; people were beginning to move back and forth. But inside, in the gloom that was still cool, he seemed isolated from all that hustle and bustle, protected from the dust and the heat. He would allow himself an hour, enjoying a second and a third cup of coffee, taking his time, giving his soul a rest in the dark quiet.

Soon enough it was over. He put on his wide-brimmed hat and adjusted the high lapels of his coat. He left two silver dollars on the table and went out into the heat and dust and turmoil. Sometime, he thought, he would like to have a little place like Roberta Blendick's over on Gunsmoke Creek — enough to keep a man busy but not enough to fight over. There wouldn't be the constant pressure of making ends meet on a big scale, of outmaneuvering the other man, of fighting off sharp-toothed rats like Summers, of fawning on dolts like Conway who dressed him down for delivering inferior beef. He snorted. Certainly it wasn't top grade beef — but it was better than anything the Indians were used to, so why the fuss? He got nine cents for second grade beef, while the Stock Growers shipped to Omaha and got eight cents for their best stuff. He supposed he would some day have to argue with the Stock Growers over that.

The sun was beating strong on his back, and he was getting worked up to the usual tension of the day. Automatically he stopped in at the post office, worked the combination on his box, and took out the mail. He glanced through the letters, took out one addressed in a woman's handwriting and postmarked at Laramie, and put it in his inside coat pocket. The rest he put in his side pocket, and went on down the street toward the surveyor's office.

He had little sympathy with Conway's idea of trying to buy out the homesteaders in the valley, but he'd might as well try. It would be cheaper to buy them out than to run them out — and perhaps more fair, if you wanted to consider that end of it. Then too the idea of putting Blake Summers between two fires gave him considerable pleasure. With Blake surrounded by Star Under a Roof cattle and hands, and pressure from Cheyenne . . . it was a pleasant thing to contemplate.

He crossed the street, his boots sinking an inch deep into the fine dust. He opened the door of the surveyor's office and meticulously took off his hat. "Good morning, Roberta."

She looked up from a handful of mail and a Geological Survey map. "Good morning, Jefferson. Sit down?"

He would. It was pleasant in here, if a bit crude. Here it was cool and quiet, and here it had always been restful, but this morning it was different: he kept seeing, in his mind's eye, his gunwhipping of Summers, and the memory of it ran through his brain and throbbed in his temples.

The soft, pleasant fragrance of Roberta's toilet water soothed him a little, and for a moment he thought he was about to recapture the feeling of restfulness and ease.

He sat stiff in the straight chair, his hat on his knees, and watched Roberta as she finished reading a letter that seemed to be connected with the map. He liked the way her dark hair coiled against her smooth skin. He liked the smoothness of her skin itself, the olive color it had acquired where it was exposed to the sun, and the soft whiteness in the hollows back of her ears.

She finished the letter and studied the map. He cleared his throat, and she looked up.

"Roberta," he said, "I want to apologize for the savage scene I must have presented in your office yesterday. I can only say that that fellow Summers has seemed to spend his lifetime getting under my skin."

She folded the letter and put it back in the envelope. "Those things are for men to settle," she said, avoiding his eyes. "Women run for the doctor — and wash up the blood."

Involuntarily he glanced at the floor. It had indeed been freshly scrubbed. "I assure you," he said, "that any further settlement between Summers and me will be made privately."

She did not answer.

"I confess it is beyond me to explain," he went on, "but the fellow has a positive genius for getting me into embarrassing situations."

She looked at him levelly. "I think I know what you are leading up to, Jefferson. Mr. Summers said you were married when he saw you last."

"I was," Tinley said, "but that has been several years ago."

She looked straight at him. "I don't like beating around the bush, Jefferson — and we have been too friendly for me to accept such an evasion even if I wanted to." She paused, her eyes not releasing him. "Let's make it a straight question, Jefferson. Are you married now?"

Damn the girl! He got up and put one hand on her shoulder. "Roberta, would you let the implied accusation of a total stranger, a drifter, come between us?"

She did not move either to or from him, and he knew she was waiting to hear the answer.

"We have gone together for a year," she reminded him, "and although I am not such a high-school girl as to take a man's intentions seriously until he declares himself, neither am I a fool. I have always had a good name in Mountain City, Jefferson, and I value it. I believe that entitles me to an answer."

He laid his hat quietly on the desk and put his other hand on her other shoulder. The fragrance of her hair made him close his eyes for an instant. Then he leaned over her, his lips close to her smooth skin.

He was astonished at the ease with which she slid out of his arms. He'd never really tried to kiss her before. He'd sensed that she was the type who would let a man kiss her when she wanted him to, and not before. If this came on their first appointment together, well and good, but if the man tried too soon, he would only jeopardize his further chances. Therefore, Tinley had been content to wait. Roberta was not, of course, the only woman in Wyoming, but she was his eventual aim, for the daughter of Amadeus Blendick, properly handled, could yet be a power in Wyoming politics.

She had turned to face him, her back to the drawing board. "I think," she said, "the answer comes before that."

Well, he could hardly blame her. She must be twenty-six or -seven. Her head was not to be turned by a stray rooster — which was all in her favor. He saw that he had delayed enough.

"The answer, Roberta, is no. I am not married. I hope to be some day, however, as soon as I get my status clear in Crazyman Valley and have something substantial to offer a prospective wife."

She studied him a long time. He didn't know whether she believed him or not. But wisely he decided not to push her. He had said what she had wanted to hear, and for a bonus, he had thrown in the tantalizing prospect of being mistress of the Washakie outfit's eighty sections of grass. He could well afford to sit back and let her think it over.

"Sorry it turned out this way, Roberta. My feeling for you gets a little too strong for me at times."

She smiled then. "Why, Jefferson, I never imagined you had such unruly emotions."

He shrugged as he turned to the door. He didn't know whether she was in earnest or whether she was ridiculing him. If he had had any reason to think it was ridicule, he would have slapped her face.

"I'm going up to the ranch for a few days," he said, his hand on the doorknob. "I'll call on you when I get back."

She nodded, her dark eyes deep and inscrutable as usual. "Goodby, Jefferson."

"Goodby, Roberta."

Back again into the sun, he went to the hotel and left his mail at his office on the second floor. Then he went down to Carthy's. There again inside the big barn, it was cool and quiet, with only the sweet, musty fragrance of a freshly opened bale of hay in his nostrils. The one-eyed Carthy kept a clean stable. Tinley stood there for a moment, heard a horse-fly buzzing, the stamp of an iron-shod hoof, and the switch of a tail against the side of a stall.

Carthy descended the straight-up-and-down ladder. He waded through the pile of straw and came up to Tinley, slapping his old hat against his leg to knock out the dust.

"Somethin', Mr. Tinley?"

"I'll want the black mare early in the morning."

"She'll be ready."

"By the way, whose roan is that with a Pronghorn brand?"

"Belongs to a gent name of Summers."

"Staying in town very long?"

"Going out tomorrow, he says. Intended to go today, but he had to wait on some bobwire."

Tinley nodded as if it were of no importance. The stable seemed to have a sour horse smell that he hadn't noticed before. He went back to see Floyd Rawson and ask about the water laws, but he didn't learn anything he didn't already know.

His mind was buzzing that night, and he was a long time getting to sleep . . .

He rode out early the next morning, and kept the mare at a lope across the sagebrush flats and into the valley. He slowed the mare to a trot until he got up to Luke Leslie's place.

He turned off by the earth dam. Tinley could see the old man leaning on the corral fence beyond the pool, and rode along the corral fence. He said, "Morning, Luke."

"Mornin'." Luke sounded sour.

Tinley found a clean place to stand, and dismounted. He threw the mare's reins over the fence and said, "How's the corn coming?"

"Corn'll be good," said Leslie, "but the arthritis is gittin' me down. Can't hardly handle my left arm at all any more." He moved it a little to show how stiff it was. "Can't even handle a fork."

"Maybe the altitude is too high for you," Tinley said.

"Maybe I'm gittin' too old."

"No, that isn't it. Why do you think I stay in town instead of up at the ranch?"

"Prob'ly because there's more women in town." Leslie cackled.

Tinley smiled quietly. "You never had trouble in Cheyenne, did you?"

"No."

"Why don't you try it back in Cheyenne for a while, then? You've got lots of friends there." He smiled. "They still talk about how you practically ran the statehouse ten years ago."

Leslie snorted; it might have meant anything. "Can't leave now. Corn crop's comin' along. Got to watch the water. And there's forty head of cattle to take care of."

"You could get a hired man," Tinley suggested, but knowing it wasn't possible to find a hired man who would take care of a place like the owner himself.

Leslie pulled a plug of Mechanic's Delight out of his hip pocket and worried off a piece with his corner teeth. He was an old man, and most of his front teeth were gone. "Don't know what to do," he admitted. "I like it up here. Proved up on my homestead and it's all mine. But what good is it? I'm all by myself — no woman, nobody to help me — and now I'm gittin' too crippled up to take care of myself even."

"How about children?" asked Tinley.

"All dead." Leslie put the plug back in his pocket. "I come up here because I like this valley this time of the morning. I was up here in the sixties huntin' Indians and I run into this valley. Early in the morning like this, when the sun lights up them yeller rocks, and it's still practically night down here in the bottom, it's sure peaceful and nice. But with this arm, I'm might' near exhausted by the time I git myself dressed."

"Maybe I could run your place for a year or so. Maybe," Tinley said as if struck by the thought, "we could get together on some kind of a deal. You know what your stuff is worth, don't you?"

Leslie stared at him. "Yes, I know what she's worth."

"What'll you take for the land?"

"Land like this is worth every cent of ten dollars an acre — every cent."

Tinley laughed. "You're away too high."

"I'm not a penny too high — and you know that yourself. Look at that corn — knee-high already. That'll make fifty bushel if it makes an ear."

"If you don't get hail."

Leslie shrank up again. "Sure. 'If this' and 'if that'."

Tinley threw the reins over the mare's neck. "Let me know if you decide to sell. I still think you and I can get together."

"Even at ten dollars an acre?"

"Maybe."

Tinley felt pretty good as he rode on up the valley. He would buy out Leslie, even at a high price. The others would be easier to deal with.

He had to get off the mare to open the gate at the Crawford fence. He pulled the post back into place with his elbow as the fulcrum of a lever, and pulled the loop of wire over it. He rode into the yard in front of the cabin, and, still sitting the mare, called out: "Hello!"

Tinley rode around the wagon shed and saw three riders, half-way to the hills, stopped to watch him. He rode up to them leisurely.

"Good morning," he said.

One of the brothers nodded.

"The Washakie place is looking for a little more land," he said. "We'd make a good price if we found somebody ready to deal."

He stared. The three brothers were all shaking their heads.

"Don't you even want to talk it over?"

Again the three heads shook in unison.

Tinley was uncomfortable. He knew stubbornness when he saw it — and he knew he had seen it. "Stop in and see me if you change your minds," he said, and rode on.

Chet White, tall and awkward, was coming out of the back door of his place, followed by Docie, almost as tall and fully as awkward.

"Somethin'?" asked Chet, stopping short.

"Just looking around," said Tinley.

"Mighty early for sight-seein'."

"It is that," Tinley admitted. "Have a cigar?"

He saw Chet's eyes light up, and held the Doña Josefa out to him. Chet took it and sniffed it, and disappeared back in the house.

Tinley sat with his hands on the saddlehorn. Docie leaned himself back against the cabin. A minute later Chet came out, puffing clouds of smoke. "Why don'tcha git down, Mr. Tinley?"

Tinley dismounted and dropped the mare's reins on the ground.

They talked about the grass, and Tinley lit one of his own cigars. They talked about Luke Leslie's corn and his arthritis, and the calf crop the preceding March. Tinley finally led up to the subject of land. Chet didn't like the idea — Tinley could see that but he kept still and listened.

"You proved up on this land, didn't you?"

"Sure. Got my papers this spring."

"It would make a nice deal if you could turn it over for two or three thousand dollars. I hear there's some open land over on Gunsmoke Creek."

Chet was studying the end of his cigar. "We-ell, I —"

The back door opened, and a woman stuck her head out. She said, "Chester White, you're not going to sell this place! We been moving all our lives, and you promised me when we come here we'd settle down and stay for keeps. I'm holdin' you to it."

The door slammed. A moment later it opened again, and a big dishpanful of water was slung in a wide, twisting arc that enclosed the entire door step. The door slammed again.

Chet looked up. "I reckon that settles that, Mr. Tinley. When she throws the dishwater like that, she means what she says. Thanks for the seegar."

Tinley's lips tightened. He'd had this farmer headed his way until the woman had butted in. He glowered for a moment at the kitchen door. Then he got to his feet. "In case you change your mind, you can see me at my office in Mountain City," he said.

"Won't be changin' it," said Chet.

Tinley rode back down the road to the big Horton place. He saw Ben Horton and his two hands heading for the hills, and so he held back the mare to give them time to get away. Then the Shoshone girl went to the barn. She came out with a bucket of corn and began to cluck at the chickens.

Tinley rode up behind her. It was mid-forenoon and he was hungry, but the solid build of the Indian girl made him forget about breakfast. He said softly, keeping his voice down so old lady Horton wouldn't hear him, "How, Soft Hands."

She whirled, her heavy black braids flying. "Oh — Mr. Tinley!"

He frowned, because she had said it pretty loud, but he got off the mare and stepped over to her quickly. They were out of sight of the hills now, and he took her in his arms.

"Put down that damn' bucket!" he growled.

She dropped it, and he pulled her close to him, his hands spread wide on her back, to feel her firm flesh through his fingers.

Then suddenly he backed away. "What's the matter with you?"

"With me?" she asked, smiling, and picked up the bucket.

He followed her. They were still hidden from the hills by the barn, and the farther they got from the house the better he liked it, for he suspected the old lady had mighty keen ears, having nothing to do but lie there and listen all day. Soft Hands stepped inside the barn to toss the bucket in the corn bin, and Tinley followed her. He pulled her body to him, and kissed her full on the mouth.

She backed away. "Mrs. is sit in the kitchen," she said.

But her ripeness had fired him. He grabbed her by the wrist and pulled her back. She struggled but he held her. She spun out of his arms and backed against the corn bin. He advanced. "You never been so scared before!" he said harshly.

She watched him but said nothing. What had got into the damn' squaw anyway? He took one big step. She tired to evade him, running for the door, but he seized her by one arm and flung her back. She crashed against the bin and fell to the floor. He stood over her, breathing harshly. He reached for her but she tried to roll away. He stopped her with his leg. She curled up, her hands and arms protecting her head.

He reached for her, but into the red haze of his brain came the sound of a wagon and team clattering up the road at a trot. He stepped outside quickly, for he knew the black mare was a giveaway. He walked over to the chicken house and pulled out a cigar, trying to appear at ease, although the blood was still hammering in his temples, and his hands were shaking as he lit the cigar.

Then he swore again, for the mule team was driven by Blake Summers. Tinley stood where he was until the wagon got past. Then he looked for Soft Hands.

But she had gone into the house, and now old man Horton, tall and thin, with a graying beard, was riding in from the hills. He had seen the mare, no doubt, and come to find out what his company wanted.

Horton rode up to the barn and tied his horse. Then he started for the house.

"Hold up a minute," said Tinley.

Horton stopped, his gray eyes suspicious.

"Have a cigar?"

"Don't smoke," said Horton.

Tinley put the cigar back in his pocket. These valley men were uncommonly hard to get along with. "How's the calf crop?" Tinley asked.

Horton stared at him. "It's for damn' sure," he said, "that you ain't askin' that out of consideration for me."

Tinley frowned. "Why not?" he asked.

"That's easy. You're for J. J. Tinley. You always was and you always will be. When you start askin' questions, I smell polecat."

"I don't think —"

"Listen," said Horton. "You see that wagon just went up the valley? That gent bought out the old Potter place, and from what I hear he's going to make it safe for small ranchers in this valley!"

Tinley didn't answer. He went over to the black mare, mounted her, and rode out of the yard without even looking for Soft Hands. So Summers had been talking down here already. Everywhere he turned was Summers.

CHAPTER EIGHT

The Crawford brothers had disappeared in the hills. Luke Leslie was not in sight. Chester White's wife, who had made up her husband's mind, had a fire going under a big kettle in the back yard — probably to make soap. Tinley trotted past the front of the cabin without looking in her direction. He had no use for women who stuck their noses into business anyway.

He held back to allow Blake Summers' wagon to keep ahead of him. He hadn't worn his pistol out here because he didn't want to give anybody an excuse to take a potshot at him, but after the gunwhipping he had given Summers, the man might be touchy.

He watched the wagon lurch and sway as it went across new ground to a spot somewhat past Potter's former cabin. He got down to open the gate, and by the time he was mounted again, Summers had stopped the wagon by a small fire. This was only a couple of hundred yards from the road and not quite as far as Tinley would have liked, but there was nothing for it but to keep his eyes straight ahead and keep the mare trotting on.

But Summers had his eye on him. The man left the wagon to walk across the grass toward the road, and

Tinley could not avoid him. Summers' man was unharnessing the mules, and Tinley saw a Winchester on the footboard of the wagon.

Tinley kept moving at a steady trot, watching Summers from the corner of his eye. Summers still wasn't wearing a hat. The bandages on his head were getting a little dirty, but they still looked white and a little grotesque, shining in the sunlight.

Summers reached a spot in the road ahead of him, and waited there. Tinley drew a deep breath and kept moving. Summers called out, "Something, Tinley?"

Tinley eyed him. "Nothing," he said.

He didn't like the look in Summers' eyes, or the grimness in Summers' face. He intended to trot on past, but Summers snatched the mare's bridle and wheeled her.

"I'm unarmed," Tinley said hastily.

"So am I," Summers said. "Are you ready to settle it this way?"

"There's nothing to settle," Tinley said. "I'm on a public road and I'm going to my ranch up the valley. I'll do my talking in the courts."

"That isn't the way you felt day before yesterday," Summers said harshly.

Tinley had it in mind that now would be a good time to settle Summers' hash — but there was Summers' man back there with a rifle.

"If you don't turn loose of that bridle," Tinley said, "there'll be trouble."

Summers' eyes narrowed. He pushed the mare's head away from him. "There's already trouble, Tinley

— lots of trouble." He paused. "There'll be more," he said flatly.

The mare backed up a step or two. "You're making a mistake," said Tinley. "You're trying to cut out the big rancher. You'll never —"

Summers came a step closer. "I'm not trying to cut out anybody, Tinley. I want room for myself and for the little men like me — Chet White, the Crawfords, Horton — all men who are just where you was before you started swinging a wide loop."

Tinley brought up his boot and kicked Summers under the chin. Summers fell back with the swing. He caught the spur of Tinley's boot and pulled him out of the saddle.

Tinley hit the ground hard, flat on his seat. Then he was up, blazing mad. He roared into Summers with both fists. Summers sidestepped and came back at him. Tinley tried to get to Summers' head; that was the soft point. But Summers kept moving. He caught Tinley flush on the chin and staggered him. Tinley shook his head and kept swinging his arms. Summers was a hazy figure before his eyes. Tinley realized he was about to go down. He reached for the hideout derringer under his arms.

But a nasal voice came through the fog and stopped him: "Leave that thing alone, Tinley, if you don't want a Winchester slug through your belly button!"

Tinley stopped. Summers hit him again. Tinley tried to fight back, but Summers was pumping fists at him. Tinley felt sick. Then Summers hit him two more on the chin. He slid into the dirt. He knew Summers tried to get him on his feet. Summers was like a man in a great rage, but Tinley knew enough to play dead. He went limp and dropped back to the ground.

After a minute he saw Summers walking away. Red Flynn still held the rifle pointed at him. He got up on his feet swaying. His forty-dollar Stetson was lying in the dirt. He shook his head to clear his eyes, then picked up the hat.

Summers' grating voice came to him. "You never were unarmed in your life, Tinley. You don't trust anybody — even your wife."

Tinley straightened. "You said that once too often already," he warned, and meant it.

"I'll say it again," said Summers. "Now get off my land!"

"This is a public road," Tinley argued.

"It'll be a public graveyard if *you* keep traveling it," Summers promised him.

Flynn growled, "What you lettin' him go for? He tried to pull a hideout gun. You could of finished him."

Summers said slowly, "I've got no proof of anything on him."

Flynn said, "I'm beginnin' to wonder why you didn't settle it in Albany County."

Tinley rode off, feeling the muzzle of that Winchester aimed at his back. He crossed Summers' last fence line and was on Washakie land. He breathed a little easier. First he felt frustrated; then he got furious. Why hadn't he let Summers reach for his pistol there in Roberta's office and then shot him down? A gunwhipping settled nothing; a bullet would.

He rounded the high yellow rocks that shielded the Washakie ranch-house from the lower valley. He rode up to the big headquarters cabin, two stories high, and got down, stomping his feet on the front porch. A Mexican came out, wearing a wide-brimmed, conical-shaped straw hat. "*Señor!*" he said.

He reached for the reins, but Tinley dropped them just before the Mexican got hold of them, and stalked into the house.

Cotton Stewart looked up from a printed form he was filling out with a pencil, and pushed his tall hat back on his white hair. "Howdy, J.J."

"Howdy, hell!" growled Tinley.

Stewart looked more closely at him. "Trouble, J.J.?"

"*Trouble!*" Tinley let Stewart see the full extent of his indignation. "How often can a man be insulted on a public road and ordered out with a Winchester at his back?"

Stewart put the pencil in his green vest pocket. "You ran into Summers down the road, then."

"I certainly did."

"You got blood on your chin, J.J."

Tinley muttered, "Those damn' Crawfords! They build their fences too tight. The gate-post slipped, and a barb raked me across the face."

Tinley walked over to the wooden filing case. He opened the bottom drawer and took out a glass and a tall bottle of bourbon. He poured himself a stiff drink and then another. "Want one?" he asked Stewart.

Stewart's eyes were on the bottle, but he shook his head — which was the ritual. Cotton Stewart could furnish his own drinking whisky; he was getting a hundred and twenty-five a month. Tinley felt for the cigars in his breast pocket. The first one he got his fingers on was shredded, and he felt for another one. That one was whole; he pulled it out and fingered it slowly, carefully, once more getting his feelings under control. He got the cigar lighted, and said:

"I want you to start putting the pressure on Summers. Make it as tough as you can on him without openly and notoriously violating the law. You know what I mean."

But Cotton Stewart was shaking his big head. "I know what you mean, J.J. I wasn't brought up in no pink tea kindygarden, but you might as well know — we been puttin' the pressure on Summers, but we been gettin' it back. Them two gents ain't greenhorns. They know how far *we* can go and they know how far *they* can go."

Tinley, now just beginning to draw an easy breath, looked at Stewart through the cigar smoke. "What happened?"

Stewart put a glass weight on the papers. "The boys reported that Summers had gone to town and left Flynn alone — and we figgered it was a good time to git in a few licks. I sent three of them down there to chouse him up a little — but he ain't the chousin' kind." He shook his big head. "I don't like these damn' Irishmen. They'd rather fight than eat."

Tinley waited, watching.

"Flynn was pulling staples out of them old posts we snaked up after Potter left, and the boys tried to ride him a little. The next thing they knew, they was lookin' down the barrel of a Winchester, and this Flynn gave them a billydoo fer us." Stewart tossed over a small, dirty piece of paper, written on heavily with a pencil. "That's a bill fer two days' board on seven steers that Flynn claims strayed onto their land, and he's holdin' the steers until we pay the board."

Tinley exploded. "What the hell *is* this! Do you mean one man can tell the Washakie what they've got to do?"

"It begins to look that way," said Stewart.

Tinley got up and paced to the window and back, puffing furiously on the cigar. "What am I payin' fifteen hands sixty dollars a month for? Not to punch cows!"

"Sure. That's fightin' pay, and they're all fightin' boys. But you forgot somethin', J.J. The last time you talked to me, you told me these two fellers were comin', and you said no rough stuff."

Tinley drew a deep breath. "All right. No rough stuff — yet. I'll give the word."

Stewart nodded slowly. "What about this board bill?"

"Let him hold 'em for a while and then try to collect."

"He'll charge us for every day he keeps 'em," Stewart reminded him.

"*Damn!*" Tinley bit the end of his cigar.

"Take it easy, J.J." Stewart's voice was soothing. "Maybe for a little while they're on top, but that's nothing to worry about. The thing is to keep an eye on them until they overstep. Until they do, I think we better watch our hole card pretty close."

"All right. Send a man down there with money. Tell him to get a receipt. Also write out a notice telling Summers to keep his fences up or we won't be responsible."

"He won't pay any attention to what we tell him."

Tinley stared at Stewart. "You're an idiot!" he shouted, and stalked out of the house.

"Tomás!"

The Mexican ran around the corner of the house.

"Get my horse! *Andale!*"

"*Sí, señor.*"

Tomás went toward the harness shed at a dog trot. You could make these Mexicans move, Tinley reflected, if you wanted them to.

He was smoking his last cigar when he rode back into Mountain City about suppertime. He left the mare at the livery and walked to the saloon, which was almost empty except for a whiskered prospector sitting at a back table and drinking himself into oblivion. Tinley went to the bar.

"Good day, Mr. Tinley?" asked the bartender, setting out a glass and a bottle.

Tinley held the small glass up to the light of the hanging kerosene lamp, then slammed it down. "Isn't there any soap back there?" he asked.

The bartender picked up the glass and stared into the bottom of it. "Sorry, Mr. Tinley." He brought up another glass, inspected it, and pushed it over. "Must have got by me somehow."

Tinley downed his drink and got out. He went over to the hotel and said to the clerk, "I want the stage to Thermopolis. Tell him to wait for me if I'm not here."

"Yes, sir, Mr. Tinley."

He went up to his office on the second floor and brushed his boots. When he came back down to the dining room. everybody had left but Floyd Rawson, behind his inevitable paper — this time *The Omaha World*. Tinley sat down at the same table. He didn't mind Rawson so much, for he could get rid of him when he wanted to.

Rawson peered at him over the paper. "You go up to the ranch today?"

Tinley nodded.

"Roast beef or pigs' knuckles," said the big waiter.

"Beef," said Tinley, "and plenty of it."

"How are things up Crazyman?" asked Rawson.

"Not bad." Tinley tucked the heavy linen napkin into his belt. "We're going to have to get water or buy some windmills, though."

"Where would you put up a windmill in the mountains?"

"On the plains."

"Still don't see why the government doesn't re-allocate that water that's earmarked for the Shoshones."

Rawson's touching on that point irritated Tinley. How many times had the pudgy lawyer seemingly picked his mind to grab an idea, and later, probably, to consider it his own? Tinley said sharply, "There's a lot of things about this country you don't see."

Rawson shut up and retired behind his paper. Then he folded the paper carefully, avoiding Tinley's eyes, and got up and left.

Tinley watched him go without comment. Rawson was a weakling.

The stage drew up to the hotel a few minutes after eight, a Concord coach pulled by four mules. Coming back, it would be upgrade all the way, and they'd have six mules.

Tinley was the only passenger. He tried to lie down in the seat and get a rest, but the road was full of ruts and the big coach body swayed and lurched. Tinley had to watch himself to keep from being rolled out on the floor.

CHAPTER NINE

They rumbled into Thermopolis about 11.30a.m., and Tinley went into the hotel. "What time does the Burlington come through?"

"South-bound?"

"Yes."

"Two-thirty-three a.m. She's generally on time."

"Is it still a flag stop?"

"No, she picks up mail. We've got three stage lines running into Thermopolis now, you know," the clerk said importantly.

Tinley looked through him. "I'm interested in the train."

The clerk's ebullience was not dampened. "Be down there at 2.30p.m. The agent will open up the station."

Tinley bought some cigars. "Anybody playing cards in the back room?"

"Usual bunch."

Tinley lit a cigar, got it going, and went back. It didn't seem like a very animated game — four men sitting around an ice cream table. All wore hats but the dealer.

The dealer took in a small pot and passed the cards. Then he looked up at Tinley. "Want a hand?"

"I'll look at a few," said Tinley.

"You're the mayor of Mountain City, aren't you?"

"Yes." Tinley pulled up a chair.

"Waitin' for the Burlington?"

"Yes."

"You'll have three hours. Ante's a quarter."

Tinley set out a handful of silver change and two ten-dollar gold pieces. "This ought to hold me till train time," he said.

"Not if I get my hands on one of them gooses," the dealer said, eyeing the gold coin.

They dealt around. Tinley's spurs kept getting tangled up in the twisted steel cross rungs of the chair, and he finally took off the spurs and put them in his coat pocket.

The game wasn't very exciting. Two of the players probably were business men; a third, Tinley judged, was a remittance man, and the fourth — the hatless one — was likely a professional gambler. Tinley lost a little and won a little. Tinley should have been able to show those yokels something about the game of stud, but the gambler was sharp. He caught Tinley bluffing on a straight he didn't fill, and won fourteen dollars on two pairs.

"You've played this game before," Tinley said.

The gambler, putting the gold piece in the pocket of his ornate vest, nodded. "A little."

Tinley had to dig for money before a fat man with a lantern looked in and called out, "Anybody going south?"

"I am," said Tinley.

"Train'll be here in ten minutes."

Tinley finished the hand, then swept his remaining money into his pocket without counting it. "See you later."

The gambler looked up. The other three were arranging their money. "Drop in any time," the gambler said.

The cordiality in the gambler's voice made Tinley feel better. He went outside and followed the fat man's lantern back to the station. The agent opened the outer door, and Tinley stepped in out of the cool night breeze coming down from the Big Horns. The agent lit a hanging kerosene lamp. Then he went to the bay window where the telegraph instrument was clicking. He adjusted an empty tobacco can over the receiver, and it magnified the clicking. He listened for a minute and then said to Tinley, "Where to, mister?"

"Otto."

It took the fat man some time to look up the tariffs, and Tinley began to wonder if he would get his ticket before the train left, but finally the agent pulled out a long green strip and began to write on it. "Change to the Wyoming & North-Western at Powder River, the Colorado & Southern at Orin Post Office, and the Union Pacific at Cheyenne. That'll be nine-thirty-eight."

He gave Tinley change for another gold piece. "You'll hit Orin tomorrow evening, and I understand they run a Pullman palace car to Cheyenne, but you'll hit Cheyenne around midnight if there's no trouble."

Tinley counted his change. The town was quiet now, an aggregation of dark shapes almost completely hidden against the deeper shadows of the mountains. This tiny little building seemed to be the only place of light and life anywhere. Tinley folded his ticket and stuck it under his hat band. "I hope this train isn't late," he said.

The fat agent was listening to the rattle of the telegraph. Presently he answered, "She left Worland on the advertised. Due here any minute."

Tinley picked up his Waldorf bag and went back outside. He heard the singing of the rails, and presently the distant twin blasts from a steam whistle. A yellow headlight appeared, like the light at the end of a tunnel, and seemed to climb as it approached, until the engine clanged past him and stopped with a screeching of brakes and blasts of steam. A man swung down from the steps of a car. He went into the station and got a handful of tissue-thin flimsies, which he put in his hat. The fat agent heaved a limp sack of mail into the baggage car. The conductor came hurrying back.

" 'Bo-oard!" he called, and Tinley climbed up the steps.

He went through a narrow passageway and past a water fountain. The train started suddenly with no warning sounds and threw him against the fountain. Then he got his feet under him and went into the car. It was lighted dimly by an oil lamp at each end. He found a red-cushioned seat with a clean spittoon. He tossed his bag into the rack above, and put his hat beside it. He looked at the time on his big gold watch. It was

2.41p.m., and the train was rolling up the Wind River Canyon. He let the back of the seat down at a longer slant. A couple of prospectors were in the far end of the car, sleeping relaxed and soundly; one of them snored with a sort of bubbling pianissimo, with a sigh about every third breath. A buxom young Mexican woman, with skin dusky and intriguing in the hollows, slept sitting up with a baby in her arms. The baby woke up and began to whimper. The mother, hardly opening her eyes, bared one breast and pushed the baby's face against it.

Tinley spent some time trying to get comfortable, but about the time he began to doze it was growing light. The Mexican baby woke up again and howled for breakfast. The mother murmured with infinite patience in her soft tongue.

That was a picture, Tinley thought: an affectionate mother. He wondered who the lucky Mexican was who had fathered this little family.

He braced himself to sit there heavy-eyed, and watch the mountains and the sunrise.

They ate in Casper, and Tinley went to the dining room. When he got back, the Mexican woman was packing sandwiches in a paper sack and finishing a cup of coffee.

At Powder River the two prospectors left them, and when they changed trains they ran into a half-drunk tie-cutting crew. At Orin the Mexican woman stayed on the North-Western while Tinley and the tie-cutters changed to the C & S. It was growing dark in the shadow of Laramie Peak, and Tinley was glad to get into a Pullman berth, even though it wouldn't be but a few hours to Cheyenne. At Cheyenne, in the squeezed-up gray stone railway station at the south edge of town, he waited till morning for the Union Pacific to take him the few miles to Otto. He walked up the one street of that small town until he saw a painted black-and-gold sign, "Water Division No. 3. Superintendent."

He went inside and up a steep, narrow stairway with a single door at the top. Inside was a big room filled with two desks, several filing cabinets, and two stenographers in crisp white shirtwaists working away at the newfangled type-writers. One of them got up and came toward him, her huge, full skirt just brushing the tops of her buttoned shoes.

"I'd like to see Mr. Blakesley," Tinley said. "Lou Blakesley."

"Mr. Blakesley is in Lander on business. Can you talk to Mr. Domseth, his assistant?"

"I want somebody who can speak with authority."

"I think you will find Mr. Domseth satisfactory. He has been connected with water affairs for a long time."

"All right. I'll talk to him."

She took him to an inner door. A gray-haired man with a stiff wing-collar and a black string tie was reading a book of statutes and making notations on a large map marked off in townships and sections.

"A gentleman to see you, sir," said the young woman, and Tinley made a mental note to hire a woman secretary as soon as he got this thing settled.

"I'm Mr. Tinley, mayor of Mountain City."

Domseth turned the book face down on the map, and leaned back. "Yes, of course. Sit down. Sorry Lou isn't here, but I may be able to help you. Of course you understand Lou is the superintendent?"

Tinley sat back in the chair. "What I'm after partly is information."

Domseth put his fingertips together.

"As you know," Tinley said, "Mountain City is a fast growing town."

"Fifteen hundred and eighty, as I recall, by the last census."

"That was eight years ago. The town has doubled since then."

"I hadn't heard that," Domseth murmured.

"Since they've been opening up more land on the reservation, and extended the stage line, we've been developing a mighty good little town up there, Mr. Domseth."

Domseth nodded appreciatively, and Tinley began to warm up. "We're already up against a shortage of water," he said, "and with the town growing as fast as it is, the situation may become serious."

"Your water now is coming from Lizard Creek, isn't it?"

"Yes, it is — and we're using practically all of that creek right now. If we hit a bad summer and the creek dries up, Mountain City is going to be in trouble, Mr. Domseth."

"That seems likely — but where do you propose to get more water?"

“Crazyman Creek is the only source I know that is available to us.”

Domseth leaned back, his eyes on the ceiling. “Your ranch is on Crazyman, isn’t it?”

“It is, but that water means little to us ranchers anyway; the way it stands now, the Indians have first right.”

“The Indians’ right is in the courts. You know, I am sure, that we could not allow any appropriation of Indian waters until that case is decided against the Indians?”

“Surely *all* of Crazyman is not appropriated.”

“Luke Leslie takes off a little water for his corn. Otherwise, I believe, most of the water that comes down the stream is vested in the Indians by treaty.”

“They haven’t used it,” Tinley argued.

“That’s true, but they are not giving up their rights. That is how the present suit started. Henry Chardon asked the board of control to declare an abandonment — which was done, everybody expecting that the Indians wouldn’t care anyway. But there’s a young Arapaho up there — appropriately named John Snow Water — who went to Harvard and got an education in law. He appealed the decision and forced Chardon to take the initiative in a suit. It was a clear case of notorious abandonment, but Snow Water appealed to the U.S. on the ground that a treaty with the Indians must be honored.”

“Isn’t it true that water rights are decided according to the laws of the state where the water is located?”

"Essentially, yes, and it seems likely that Snow Water will lose his appeal, but Wyoming was not a state at the time of the treaty, and right now we can do nothing."

Tinley took a deep breath. "There's one source of water that isn't overappropriated," he said. "That's the flood water. What's to keep Mountain City from building a dam to impound the flood waters each spring?"

Domseth raised his eyebrows. "There's nothing to keep you from it," he said, "but you might find yourselves with an empty dam on your hands."

"For what reason?"

"I am familiar with the water in Crazyman Valley," said Domseth. "The meadow in the bottom of the valley is made rich by the overflow of water every spring; it fills the valley and carries rich silt and moisture. That's why the grass in the valley is so fine. No" — he shook his head — "I'm afraid you're in trouble there. I admit it is a point that has not been determined by the courts, but the general opinion among water men is that usage of the grass is the same as use of the water."

Tinley leaned forward. "Isn't municipal use a preferred use in Wyoming?"

Domseth studied him as he considered this. "Yes, of course. But you would have to condemn the present use of the overflow waters — and I'm sure there would be a fight over that, for Crazyman would be worthless without the overflow."

Tinley got up. "As far as this office is concerned, then, there is nothing to be done."

"I'm afraid that's the way it looks to me, Mr. Tinley. Of course if Lou Blakesley —"

"Never mind, I'm sure you reflect Blakesley's opinion. But there are other ways to skin a cat, Mr. Domseth."

"Undoubtedly." Domseth got up and shook hands. "Good luck," he said.

CHAPTER TEN

Tinley went out and had a couple of drinks. Undoubtedly there were other ways — but what other ways? So far everything had been going wrong for him. Perhaps it was time to move and move hard.

He found it was six hours until an east-bound train, so he went to the livery and engaged a ride in a light wagon. He got into Cheyenne in the late afternoon, and went down a side street to a sign that said, "Homer Mohr, Attorney." The sign was old and weather-beaten, and the office inside looked about the same. There was no stenographer in sight, and no note to indicate when Homer Mohr would be back. Tinley lit a cigar and made up his mind to wait.

He must have gone to sleep, for he heard a dry voice saying, "See you made yourself comfortable."

He glanced at his cigar and saw that it had gone out. He looked up at a tall, gangling man with long black mustaches and a soft black hat. His coat and vest were food-stained down the front and wrinkled from long lack of pressing. Tinley said, "You haven't changed in ten years."

A crafty look came over Mohr's face, then passed. "Were you in Albany County ten years ago?"

"Yes."

Mohr nodded. "Jeff Tinley, aren't you?"

Tinley stood up and shook hands. He gave Mohr a cigar, and they both sat down.

"Got a place up in the Owl Creek Mountains, haven't you?"

"Yes."

Mohr eyed him through a cloud of smoke. "Trouble?"

"A little."

"Over what?"

"Water."

Mohr took the cigar out of his mouth. "Water's a touchy subject," he observed.

Tinley didn't comment. He had expected that answer. It was a part of Mohr's strategy, and Tinley countered with some of his own. "Maybe I should see Burdick, the state chairman."

Mohr looked at him. "You aren't that big a fool," he said. "Strong arm stuff won't get you anywhere. Sure, any state chairman has influence, but he can't use it in a deal like this. You may have to go through the state board of control to the courts. And that's no place for amateurs."

"You aren't trying to tell me the courts can't be touched, are you?"

Mohr's eyes almost closed. "You know better than that. But you don't barge into court with a stack of yellowbacks and start telling them what to do. These judges have principles. If they suspect that a man is trying to buy them, he won't have any luck at all."

"How —"

Homer Mohr gave him a slow look. "If you knew the answer to that," he said, "you wouldn't be here." He puffed out a cloud of smoke around his head. "I'll tell you this much: like I said, influencing a decision is not just a matter of laying down so much money. You've got to know where to put it. If you want to influence a judge, you get to him through a friend of his. And maybe this friend is hard to get to." He thought about it a while. "Why don't you come back in three days?"

Tinley nodded slowly. "All right, I'll come back in three days." He took his bag down to the station and asked, "When is the next train for Laramie?"

"There's a mixed local leaves at 9.40p.m. Get you into Laramie at 11.58p.m."

"That will take forever," Tinley grumbled.

"It's a local. Drops freight off as it goes along. Or you can catch the through train at 5.10 in the morning."

Tinley felt like fighting with somebody, for this was a trip he didn't want to make anyway. But he thought better of it and tossed out two silver dollars.

At Laramie the next morning he went to the livery stable.

"Morning, Mr. Tinley. How you this fine morning?"

"Good as can be expected," Tinley said shortly.

"Want a saddle horse?"

"Yes."

"How are things going up at Mountain City?"

Tinley looked at him sharply. "Fair."

The man led a bay horse out by its halter. "I hear the town is booming."

"Don't believe all you hear," Tinley advised him.

He rode up into Snowy Range and turned off on a wagon road past the Little Laramie River. By evening he was on the Laramie Plains — a wide, rolling area on top of the mountains. The altitude was about 9,000 feet, and he frequently had to give the horse a breather. He went over a ridge that was hardly more than a swell, and followed the road down the other side. A small log cabin, set in a clearing at the edge of the pine forest, showed up. A yellow light appeared in a window before he got there. A woman's voice was heard occasionally.

Tinley opened the last gate, went through, and closed it. He looked with distaste at the outbuildings, which needed paint; the chinking was falling from between the logs of the house. Tinley rode by the house, saw an older girl opening the oven of a coal stove while a small boy sat at the table and hammered with his fists. Tinley rode on to the barn and dismounted. He dropped the reins on the ground, and went in. He heard a cow crunching hay between its molars with apparently placid relish; he smelled the freshly opened bale, and heard the alternate streams of milk beating into a pail. He stood there for a moment, adversely affected by all these homely things, but finally he said, "Vera."

The steady pumping of the milk stopped abruptly. "Jeff!" said a glad voice, and a moment later a woman came running across the barn.

She stumbled as she fell against him. “Jeff!” she said again, and hugged him hard — almost desperately, it seemed to him. Her head was against his chest, and he put his arms around her because she would complain if he didn’t.

“I’m *so* glad you’ve come,” she said finally.

“Any trouble?” he asked her.

“We lost two calves to a bear last month. I’ve carried the rifle, looking for him, and I make the children stay in at night, but — oh, Jeff, it’s hard for a woman to run a place like this without any help.”

“I know,” he said. “It won’t be much longer.”

“You said that six years ago, Jeff.”

He patted her shoulder briefly. “We’ve had some bad winters up north of the reservation. I have to feed my stock all winter, and then when summer comes the snow runs off with the chinook winds and leaves nothing but sagebrush and prickly pear.”

She backed away, looking up at him. “I’ll finish the milking,” she said. “Stay close to me until I get through. Will you?”

“Yes, of course.” He knew at once he had answered testily, and he reminded himself to be careful of that.

After supper he looked over her dutifully kept accounts. Bookkeeping was not one of Vera’s strong points, but he saw that she was making the place pay its own way. While the two older girls were washing and drying the supper dishes, and Vera was baking bread for the next day — “I know how you like fresh light bread, Jeff, and if you had let me know you were coming!” — he worked on her figures so as not to show too much of a balance in the bank. When he got back to Cheyenne, he would stop and draw out the surplus; that way she wasn't likely to gather up the kids and visit him in Mountain City.

That was the most distasteful thing he could look forward to: Vera's dragging those four kids into Mountain City for a visit.

Still later, with the children in bed, Vera brought out a bottle of wine. "I splurged the last time I was in Laramie," she confessed, "thinking of the next time you would be home. It's sherry too, the kind you like."

He needed a drink of whisky, but he didn't dare say so. They had shared a bottle of wine in their courting days, and he had allowed Vera to think ever since that he never drank anything stronger than wine. So he made up his mind now to endure it, although Vera's little intimacies were reaching a grueling stage.

She poured a glass for each of them, and put the bottle away in the top of the cupboard, then sat across the table and watched him, her deep red hair glowing in the lamplight, her blue eyes watching his every move. "I can't get enough of you," she said again and again, and he looked at her smallness and compactness and wondered how it was possible for such a small woman to have so much energy. She had been up since three-thirty, had ridden the range all day, depending on the oldest girl to take care of the kids, but now she sat across the table from him, and her eyes sparkled and she no longer even looked tired.

"How long can you stay, Jeff? A week?"

He tasted the wine and shook his head as he set down the glass. "I have to pull out day after tomorrow," he said. "Have to do some financing in Cheyenne and get back to Mountain City. We've had trouble with rustlers," he added, "and with only two or three men I can't afford to stay away so long."

"You never stay long enough for me to get acquainted with you," she said, complaining.

"That's the way life is. Some people are lucky. The rest of us have to work and sacrifice to make a living."

She sipped her wine, her eyes not leaving his face. A quick change then came over her features. "I heard from Tommie yesterday," she said.

He studied his wine. Tommie was not a pleasant subject for him. "How is he?" he asked at last.

"All right, I suppose. He was made a trusty in the library, and he likes that, for he can read." Suddenly the words poured out. "Oh, Jeff, it's terrible that a twenty-year-old has to be in prison when he didn't really do any more than a thousand other boys do."

He heard the near-sobs in her voice, and kept discreetly silent.

"He will come up for parole in two years." Vera sounded hopeful.

"These five years won't hurt him," Tinley said with easy assurance. "He'll learn that the law is not a thing to be taken lightly — and that's an important lesson for any boy."

"It was a boy's prank," she insisted, "and Olcott knew it. He prosecuted Tommie because he and you were on bad terms."

Tinley said, "That's a hard thing to say of a man."

"It wouldn't have happened if you had been home," she said as she had said a hundred times before. "He never liked you and he was angry with me because I wouldn't let him come in the house at night, so he took it out on Tommie — and all Tommie did was catch up one of his horses to ride to Laramie and back."

Tinley tossed off the wine. "Horse stealing is a serious offense in cattle country," he pointed out.

But she shook her head stubbornly. "He wouldn't have done it if you had been here, Jeff."

He said testily, "I'm doing my very best."

She filled his glass again. Then abruptly she looked across the table at him. "Jeff, you're not interested in another woman, are you?"

He frowned. "What are you talking about?"

"You're not glad to be home any more — even when it's been a long time." She was suddenly intense. "Jeff, this is no way to live." She glanced toward the children's bedroom and saw that the door was closed. "I can't keep this up much longer."

He stared coldly at her, suddenly warned. "If you do anything precipitate," he told her, "I'll leave the country."

Tears began to fall from her cheeks onto the oilcloth. "Jeff, you couldn't do anything like that!"

"I am the master in my own house," he said. "When the time comes that I am not, it is time for me to leave."

She put her head in her arms and sobbed, almost without sound. Her shoulders shook for a moment, and tears stained the forearm of her blue wool shirt. He knew she wanted him to touch her, but he'd be damned if he was going to be railroaded.

Finally she raised her head and looked at him through reddened eyes. "Jeff, I'll do anything," she said. "I'll stay out here a million miles from nowhere and run the ranch and do the best I can, if you will just get busy and make a home for us so we can all be together. Four children we've got, Jeff. They're yours as much as mine. I can't raise them by myself, Jeff. I swear I can't. There are three girls growing up. Helen is almost fourteen, and she does a woman's work already. They've got to have a father, Jeff, and a home like other kids. They need a father to keep them out of trouble."

"If they're going to get in trouble," he said, "they'll do it whether they have a father or not. But if it makes you feel better, I'm working hard. I want to establish a home just as much as you do. Do you think it's any fun for me to live alone?"

"Oh, Jeff!"

That always got her. She was in his arms, in his lap, her face in the hollow of his shoulder. He took a deep breath. He got up, carrying her. He leaned over and blew out the light.

CHAPTER ELEVEN

Two days later Tinley was back in Cheyenne. The first thing he did was to withdraw five hundred dollars to keep her balance from getting too large. Since the statements were sent to Mountain City, she would not know about the withdrawal.

When he had gone over her account book with her and pointed out the shortage, she had become alarmed, for she had just bought two windmills and tanks, and she asked him to send her some money, but he claimed he didn't have it, and compromised by giving her forty dollars in cash. He wasn't worried; she always managed, no matter how little it was. The only thing that worried him was a surplus.

Then he went around to Homer Mohr's office.

The man sat back in his swivel chair, with his feet up on his overloaded desk and his soft black hat pushed to the back of his head. "Come in, Tinley."

Tinley offered him a cigar. Mohr took it, sniffed it, bit off one end and blew it in the general direction of the spittoon. He struck a match on the under side of the desk and lit the cigar. Tinley sat down and lit one of his own.

Presently Mohr looked up. "I've done some investigating into the possibility of water for Mountain City," he said. "Now that we've come this far, let's understand each other."

Tinley stayed silent.

"What you really want," Mohr said, puffing, "is to freeze out the homesteaders in Crazyman Valley. Isn't that the story?"

Tinley cleared his throat. He shrugged. "The homesteaders are not my responsibility," he said.

Mohr nodded slowly, his dark eyes staying on Tinley's. Finally he got up. The swivel chair squeaked as the back wobbled.

"Let's go make a call," he said.

Tinley went with him, Mohr blowing out great clouds of cigar smoke. They walked four blocks in the direction of the statehouse. Then Mohr turned in at a three-story building that said, "Capitol Hotel." He led the way past the desk and took an ancient open-work elevator to the third floor. He went down a hall and turned right, then right again. He knocked at a door. When it was opened he went in. Tinley followed.

Tinley got a look at the man who had opened the door. He was a small man and wore a derby hat and a silk shirt with purple sleeve garters.

Mohr opened an inner door and pushed it in. "Evening, Jason."

A wheezy voice said, "Evening, gents. 'Light and sit."

Tinley saw a medium size man, fat all over, from pudgy legs to a neck that seemed to overflow his low, stiff collar in all directions. The collar had been unbuttoned and now hung agape, revealing the gold button in the shirt band, but still the man's neck overflowed the collar.

"Drink?" asked the wheezy voice.

Tinley nodded. Mohr found a couple of cloudy glasses and poured them full from a bottle that he took from a rolltop desk. The fat man sat in a rocker, with his feet across a straight chair, and waited for them to drink.

Finally Mohr said, "This is Jason Yarborough."

The big man nodded. "You're Tinley, I take it."

"Yes." Tinley was not entirely pleased. He had expected to see at least the Republican state chairman.

Yarborough said to Mohr, "That's a mighty good cigar."

Mohr looked at Tinley. Tinley handed one over and lit it; then he lit one for himself.

"Have another drink," said Yarborough.

It was good bourbon, anyway. The room began to lose its reek of cigar smoke and stale whisky. Tinley had another.

Finally Yarborough said, "I been looking into your situation, Tinley. It seems to me the town of Mountain City has got to be taken care of."

Tinley glanced at the big man.

"We can't have a state without towns," said Yarborough, "and towns have got to have water."

"Have another drink," said Mohr.

"In fact," said Yarborough, coughing, "I feel we should take a long-range view of this matter."

Tinley inspected his cigar, waiting.

"Obviously," said Yarborough, "Mountain City will continue to grow. There are some who think Mountain City will become the metropolis of the northwestern part of the state."

Tinley nodded. He began to see how this was going — and it was all to the good.

"How many people will there be in Mountain City in, say, twenty years?"

Tinley started to answer, but Yarborough went on. "I'd say, at the rate of growth in the last five years, you can expect twenty-five thousand population." He had another drink. "We don't like to be accused of short-term planning," he said. "As long as we are preparing for the future, why not do it right?"

"We have to look out for the future," Tinley agreed.

There was more talk of the same kind, while the smoke got thicker and thicker in the room, and the smell of whisky seemed to disappear entirely. Finally Yarborough, not having moved from his chair, said, "Well, Mr. Tinley, we'll do our best for you. Give my regards to Cotton Stewart."

Tinley stared for an instant. Then he nodded. "I will."

They went out through the other room. Homer Mohr opened the outer door and they went down the hall.

"I'll walk over to your hotel with you," said Mohr as they descended in the elevator.

"All right."

The night air, sweeping across the rolling plains from the east, was refreshing. They walked southeast, to the business part of town, and Tinley found his hotel. Mohr followed him to his room. "Got any whisky?" he asked.

"I'll get some."

Tinley went down to the desk and sent a bellboy for a quart of bourbon. He went back upstairs and opened the window. The bellboy came up, and Mohr had a drink from the bottle.

"You heard what Jason said?"

"Yes, I heard it."

"He knew what he could do, but he wanted to look at you before he stuck his neck out. These things are touchy, you know."

"I know. I suppose you decided how much it would cost."

"Yes." Mohr had another drink.

Tinley had never seen men pour booze down like Mohr and Yarborough without showing any effects. He stayed near the window.

Mohr went on. "Some of the little men will have to be paid off directly. Some will do what Yarborough asks. The bigger men are harder to get to." He paused.

Tinley waited. He knew what all this was leading up to.

"It'll cost you twenty-five thousand," Mohr said.

Tinley hesitated. He hadn't expected that stiff a price.

"Water rights," Mohr murmured, "are hard to get to. But they're worth a lot of money when you get them."

Tinley thought it over. He knew the price was not too high for what he wanted, but it annoyed him that he had to pay money to get rid of men like Blake

Summers. He knew also, however, that he had no choice. He lit a cigar for himself, carefully biting off the end and blowing it out of the window, watching the blue smoke spiral up toward the kerosene lamp on the wall. "I'll give twenty thousand," he said at last.

Mohr, carrying the bottle, got up and went to the door. Tinley said nothing. After all, he reasoned, they wanted the money as much as he wanted the water.

Mohr turned at the door. "Jason doesn't like a welsher," he said. "If I was to tell him you even argued about the money, he wouldn't have anything to do with it."

"How do I even know he can get it done for me?"

"Why did you come to me in the first place?" He waited a moment. "You knew I could get what you wanted. Isn't that it?"

Tinley eyed him. Mohr's eyes weren't even open.

"I've done what you asked. I've spent my time. We can call it off now, and I'll send you a statement for one thousand dollars for investigating the priority of water rights on Crazyman."

Tinley's jaw hardened. He would like to lay the man out with a scantling, for Mohr had not only called his bluff but he had raised it — and now he was rubbing it in.

Mohr started on through the door. Tinley let him get through before he stopped him. "How do you want it?" he asked.

Mohr took another drink from the bottle. He came back inside and closed the door. "You don't have to pay it all now. In fact, we won't take it all now, for amounts like that attract too much attention. Give me a check for $3,000."

Tinley frowned. "A check for $3,000?"

"Endorse it 'Fee for investigating water priorities.' "

Tinley's eyes narrowed. Mohr looked at him steadily. "When are you going back to Mountain City?"

"Tomorrow."

"I'll meet you at the train tomorrow afternoon. You have $2,000 in gold for me then."

"That's five," said Tinley.

"That leaves twenty. Give me the check now."

Tinley opened the writing desk. There was hotel stationery and an ink-well inside, and two steel-pointed pens. He sat down and took a check out of the money folder in his inside pocket. "Make it out to you?" he asked without turning around.

"That's right."

For a moment there was only the scratchy sound of a steel pen point; then he signed with a flourish, and heard the whisky bottle glug as it was turned bottom down again. He blotted the check and turned in the chair. He extended the check to Mohr.

Mohr took it. He scrutinized it, then looked at the back. "You forgot to endorse it," he said.

Tinley took it back and endorsed it.

Mohr looked it over and nodded. He folded it and put it in his pocket. "Now," he said, "I'm holding your check, endorsed in your own handwriting — which would be enough to send you to the pen if you open your mouth."

Tinley swallowed. "Aren't you going to cash it?"

"Not unless I cash it in court."

Tinley took a harsh breath. "You're running this pretty high-handed."

"There's no other way to run a deal like this. We don't want anybody to back down at the last minute, and we don't want anybody to holler. This check is insurance against both. If you ever say a word, you'll be talking yourself into prison."

"While you —"

"You'd have a hard time," said Mohr, "finding a lawyer willing to buck Jason Yarborough."

"How are you going to arrange this?"

"Never mind. Just get the money ready. When we have the job done, I'll come to Mountain City to collect $23,000. I expect you to have it in cash, and gather it as you go along, so as not to attract attention."

"How long do I have?"

"You better be ready in three or four months."

Tinley said coldly, "How can a man get together that much cash in three months without attracting attention?"

"That's up to you," said Mohr.

"How will I know you're doing me some good?"

"You'll know. There won't be any doubt about it. I won't come for the money until you do know."

"All right. I'll have $2,000 in gold at the train tomorrow."

"That's right. Follow instructions. Mind your own business. Get back to Mountain City. Stay away from Cheyenne. And have the money ready when I come for it."

He opened the door and went through.

“Wait a minute,” said Tinley.

Mohr came back. He was beginning to stagger a little.

“That bottle of whisky,” Tinley said flintily, “was not included in the deal.”

Mohr looked at him and sneered. He took another drink out of the bottle and then hurled it through the open window. Tinley heard it shatter on the bricks below.

CHAPTER TWELVE

Old man Horton's peach tree was bearing golden fruit by the time Blake Summers began to get squared away on his section. It was hardly believable that the summer was almost gone, but, when he looked around him, there was plenty of evidence. They had run their fence and had maintained it. They had snaked logs down from the hills and put up a fair-sized cabin with broadaxes and spikes.

"I sure don't know what you're buildin' it so big for," Red Flynn said, "unless you're plannin' to raise a big family."

Blake began to rummage for the makin's with his forefingers in his vest pockets. "A man doesn't have to *plan* a family," he reminded Red. "When the right girl comes along, the family follows."

"You got any idea who the right one is?"

"Well, no." Blake quit hunting for the makin's and concentrated on the bacon he was cooking over the fireplace.

"You spent plenty of time helping that surveyor woman."

Blake's upper lids lowered a little. "Wouldn't you, if you got a chance?"

"You damn tootin'."

"Well?"

They repaired the corral, which Blake could not quite see why Tinley's men had left whole unless Tinley expected to use it sometime, and watched over the spring calves, for wolves were plentiful, and toward the end of summer a bear wandered down from the mountains. Together they cornered the animal over the carcass of a newly killed calf, and later they spread the hide on the outside wall of the cabin.

"Is that to scare the other bears?" asked Red.

"It's to keep out the winter wind," said Blake.

Red looked upvalley toward Washakie land. "I hope we'll be here to see it."

"They haven't bothered us all summer," Blake pointed out.

Red nodded. "I'd rather be choused up a little now and then. It keeps a man sharp. This way you get lazy — and first thing you know, they land on you with all four feet, and you're asleep."

Blake looked at him soberly. "I feel the same way about the Washakie outfit — as if they're sitting back waiting to hit us with everything in the book."

"Maybe they'll ride down on us some night with about sixty rifles blazing."

"Maybe. He's got something up his sleeve, for a man like Tinley doesn't turn Sunday school all of a sudden. He's a born throat-cutter and always will be. The only thing is" — Blake's eye corners were wrinkled — "how will he do it and when will it come?"

Blake had made friends with the homesteaders, too. Chet White — impelled, most likely, by his plain but rather attractive wife — had lined up with Blake, and they had had some good sessions at night, in one cabin or the other.

Blake hired Docie to help him with the cabin, and Docie proved not only industrious but talkative when he got over his shyness. "Pappy says this was no place for a man with eight young'uns," he said.

"A man with a mess of kids," Blake noted, "has got to play 'em close to his vest. Kids make a difference. You can't go around sticking your neck out when you know that many mouths are waiting to be fed three times a day."

"I think," Docie said, picking up his end of a short log, "I'd rather be like you."

Blake, with his end of the log on his shoulder, stared at the tall boy. "Now what in h— what in the world do you want to be like me for?"

"Because you're strong, and you're not afraid of anybody."

After an instant Blake said, "Come on now, heave it up there, and be sure the notches fall right."

"I heard about how you fought Mr. Tinley three times in two days."

"Fighting is one thing," said Blake. "Maybe you never heard. Tinley won two of those fights."

But Docie was filled with the unshakeable convictions of youth. "You didn't run away, though," he said, his blue eyes shining.

* * *

Blake made a trip to Mountain City the next day. On the way he saw somebody irrigating Luke Leslie's corn, and stopped to say howdy. The man straightened up from his ditching, and Blake saw that it was one of the silent Crawford brothers.

"What happened to Luke?" Blake asked. "He sick?"

The Crawford brother straightened up. He was a big man, solid as a Belgian draft horse and twice as stolid. "He's gone to Cheyenne," he said.

Blake had reined the roan around. "His arthritis gettin' him down?"

"Don't know," said Crawford. "Don't know at all. He asked if we could watch his corn."

Blake rode on. Old man Horton was picking the first ripe peaches and handing them down to Soft Hands.

"Going to make a little brandy?" Blake asked.

"Might be," said Horton. "Reckon a little peach brandy might come in nice these long winter even's."

"I reckon." Blake watched the Indian girl stretch her arm upward to take the fruit, and Blake inhaled a full, deep breath. No wonder John Wall came down out of the hills every night.

But that was Wall's business — and Soft Hands', Blake reflected as he rode out on the sagebrush flats toward Mountain City. A flight of sagehens got up ahead of him with a roar, and he made a mental note to get Red Flynn's old shotgun and come up here. The spring hens were three-quarters grown and almost as plump and solid as Soft Hands.

He left his horse at the watering trough in Mountain City, and went across to the corner to see Perry Miller.

The bald-headed little banker seemed glad to see him. He shook hands and invited him back to his desk and offered him a cigar.

"Haven't had one of these in a long time," he said, sniffing it hungrily.

The banker's goatee and his rabbit-fur tufts of whiskers seemed to stick straight out from his face as he held a match to his own cigar. Blake was licking the end of his, and now he bit off the end. "I really shouldn't smoke this," he said. "My man has stayed up there all summer and hasn't been in town once, and it makes me feel a little guilty."

The banker opened a drawer and took out two more. "Here, take these along. Give one to Flynn and smoke one yourself, some night when you've got nothing to do but think."

Blake shook his head. "Nope. I wasn't hinting. I'll pick up a couple for Red over at the saloon."

"Fiddlesticks! You won't find anything like this between here and Casper."

Blake sniffed the fragrant smoke. "I hadn't ought to," he said. "I haven't given you any business at all yet."

"You will," Perry Miller said cheerfully, "one way or another. Anyway, a man who can keep the Washakie outfit under his thumb the way you have, has got a treat coming."

Blake frowned worriedly. "I really don't like this situation," he said. "I knew Tinley down in Albany County, and I know doggone well this whole thing is going to bust wide open. It's only a question of time."

He drew on the cigar. "What I can't figure is what's holding him up."

The banker leaned back. "J. J. Tinley is a shrewd man," he observed.

Blake nodded. "I'm here on business this time. My credit is used up, and I need some money for winter feed."

"How much?"

"About four hundred, to start with. If the winter is a hard one, it could go a couple hundred more."

Miller nodded. "You've put eleven hundred cash into that place besides your stock. There's no mortgage on it, is there?"

"Not yet."

"Give me a chattel on forty head, and tell them down at the feed store I said to credit you with four hundred."

"Forty head? Those cattle are worth more than ten dollars a head."

"They aren't if they get caught in a snowstorm and you lose half of them," said Miller.

"All right." Blake got up. "I won't be hauling any out today. I'll bring the wagon in the latter part of the week."

"Any time. The interest starts when you get the cake."

"Good enough."

"I'll have the mortgage ready when you come back."

Blake went in and had a drink, feeling pretty good. He had a tight cabin, a nice, strong crop of calves, and credit at the bank. He bought a pint of Madison Club

— Red would like that with his cigar — and was slipping it into his hip pocket when he looked into the mirror and saw the rolled-up gun-belt just under the mahogany bar. "Somebody been dehorned?" he asked the bartender.

The man saw what Blake meant, and shook his head. "That's Mr. Tinley's. He leaves it here when he's not using it."

Blake thought that over on another drink. Then he walked down the street to the surveyor's office.

But he was disappointed there. The door was locked. It was considerably before noon, so he went into the harness shop next door, into a smell of fresh leather and tanning fluid. "I was looking for Miss Blendick."

A hunch-backed old man, almost hidden beneath a row of exquisite hand-tooled saddles riding a tree, cackled a little. "Never see a young feller around Mountain City that wasn't. Would myself if I was sixty years younger."

Blake grinned. "Her place is locked. Do you have any idea where she's gone?"

"She said if anybody came looking for her, she was up on Poison Mountain."

He went up to the livery and asked Carthy about Poison Mountain.

"That's just over the ridge from you and up a ways. In the reservation, if I rightly remember. You got business with the Indians?"

"How would you reach it?" asked Blake.

"Ride out through the sagebrush about four mile. You remember a road turns off to the right?"

"Yes."

"Goes through the old Seven X range. They got cleaned out in the winter of '88; you'll see the bones up there."

"How far up?"

"Keep up the valley until you pass the ranch-house. There may be some Indians living in the headquarters house, but keep on going. You'll see Poison Mountain off to your left. There's a long spur sticks out. You climb that and you can go straight up the mountain."

"Thanks."

Blake was impatient to get away. He swung the roan under him and lit out for the sagebrush flats. He came to the spur and climbed it. He let the roan take a breather while he looked the mountain over. He rode along the base of the mountain looking for sign, but didn't find any. He wondered what on earth Roberta Blendick was surveying up there. The mountain was too steep for cattle, and there wasn't any grass.

He came to a deep canyon and rode along it, but there was no trail and there didn't seem to be any way around. It became more like a gorge as it climbed the mountain. Blake turned back and went down about half a mile, still without finding any sign.

He was a little below the trail where he had brought his herd over, from the looks of the valley. He started to angle the roan down the slope when a clear voice called from below him: "Lower, please."

He stopped the roan and studied the mountainside for a moment. Then he saw Roberta Blendick, dressed in a felt hat, an Indian buckskin jacket, and men's pants tucked into cowboy boots, braced with her feet apart, sighting into her surveyor's transit and waving both arms toward the ground.

He dismounted, careful to make plenty of noise so as not to frighten her. She must have heard him, but she did not look back.

"There. That's it. Hold it right there." She made a notation in a small notebook. Then she cupped her hands and called. "Drive a stake there!"

Blake went down the steep grade with the sides of his boots sliding on the pine needles. She checked the reading on the transit again, looked at the level, and wrote in the book. Then she turned just as he broke out into the open. "Oh, Mr. Summers!"

Her voice was like the song of a meadowlark, and it took him by surprise. She had been so cool and business-like back in Mountain City, and now here, without warning, she sounded as if he was a long-lost friend.

"Howdy, ma'am."

"This is an odd place for you to be riding, Mr. Summers. Have some of your cattle strayed up here?"

"No, ma'am," he said. "I reckon I strayed off up here by myself."

"It's quite a way to stray," she said, "especially since you must have come from over the mountain."

"Well, not so far," he said, "because I knew what I was looking for."

"A nice elk, perhaps?"

He grinned. "No, ma'am. I heard you were up here on business, and I just thought I'd ride by and see how you were getting along. You see," he said earnestly, "I have reason to believe that reservation land is dangerous for some people."

"Not for me, Mr. Summers. John Wall and I understand each other very well since he found out I had no desire to live in his teepee."

He realized he had taken off his big hat. Now he looked down at her. She looked nice in a man's hat. The heavy coils of black hair could hardly go under it, but she had turned up the brim in front — probably to keep it from touching the transit — and it made a nice frame for her oval face and her brown eyes that were always alive, always watching, questioning, laughing, or dancing. He put his hat on his head. "Are you opposed to matrimony, ma'am?"

She laughed. "Hardly. But I'm not in *that* big a hurry."

"You don't aim to run contour lines all your life, do you, ma'am?"

She studied him curiously. "How do you know I'm running contour lines?"

He smiled. "I've been on surveying parties a time or two."

"Apparently you have." She seemed thoughtful.

The man had driven the stake, the blows of the hand axe ringing across the slope.

"Who's that helping you with the rods?" Blake asked.

"That's Docie White. He and I get along well together."

"He's a good boy," Blake said.

She was motioning Docie with both hands held high above her head. He kept going.

"Where's your bench mark, ma'am?"

She pointed. "Up there on the big flat rock."

He scrambled up an almost vertical hillside, and found a lead plate set in the top of the rock. It said: "43° 25′ N. 108° 20′ W. 8515 Ft." The date of the reading was obscured.

He went back down. It was very pleasant there on the slope, but presently the high peak threw the side of the valley in shadow. He helped her pack the transit and sling the table and instrument on a mule.

They heard Docie coming through the pines. The thick carpet of needles gave out a soft crunching as he walked.

"It's been very pleasant helping you, ma'am," said Blake.

"It's been nice to have you, Mr. Summers."

"By the way, you never did tell me what you were running contour lines up here for."

She looked at him. Her mouth opened slowly, and it was a mouth made for kissing, but he waited. "I —"

Docie yelled something. Roberta Blendick looked up. "Somebody followed you over the mountain," she said.

Unconsciously Blake put his hand on the butt of his .44.

But the man who came through the pass was Red Flynn, riding the lathered dun mustang. "You give me a hell of a time!" he exploded, and then took a second look at Roberta. "Beg pardon, ma'am. I didn't see you, wearin' men's clothes and all."

"Did Carthy tell you where I was headed?"

"Yeah. Listen, Blake. There's news from Mountain City — bad news! Chet White rode into town right after you, and he heard it, but he couldn't find you."

Blake took a breath of the thin air. "Bad news?"

Roberta was quiet. Docie had come up and was watching Red with a frown on his face.

"The state water board has reclassified a big bunch of water on Crazyman."

Blake frowned. "Reclassified? How?"

"They changed it from irrigation to municipal use."

"All right — and municipal is a preferred use," said Blake.

"You're mighty right it is."

Blake said slowly. "That's nothing to get het up about. Nobody was irrigating anyway but old man Leslie — and he wasn't much." But he knew from Red's face that something was wrong with that answer.

Red put out a thick arm in a gray flannel sleeve sour with sweat, and tapped Blake on the chest. "They got us goin' and comin', Blake. You know what Chet says?"

"No."

"He says we were using the water for irrigation, because the valley depends on the spring overflow for its grass. Chet claims the grass wouldn't be worth a d— beg pardon, ma'am — he claims the valley wouldn't be worth a whoop without the spring overflow. That's called an uncontrolled use, but just the same we gotta have it."

"Wait a minute, now. They can't do that. Western water rights all go by use — and we've had prior use."

"I'm tryin' to tell you, Blake, they've reclassified the water for municipal use, and that ranks over irrigation just like three Kings rank over two pair."

"How —" Blake began. Then he turned slowly to Roberta. "Is that right, ma'am? Do you know the water law?"

Her face was unreasonably white around her dark eyes.

"I don't know water law," she said. "Nobody really knows it, because a lot of it hasn't been decided yet. But what he says sounds right to me."

The town — which meant Tinley — was taking over the water!

CHAPTER THIRTEEN

Blake got on the roan without a word. When he was mounted he looked at Roberta. "I hope you'll excuse me, miss. This sounds like something that needs taking care of."

She answered, "If you're going down the valley, we may as well all go together."

Blake looked down toward the Washakie layout with farseeing eyes. "I got a hunch we could ride through their front yard without them even seeing us," he said. "This is why they been leaving us alone all summer. Tinley had this up his sleeve all the time."

"You don't like Mr. Tinley, do you?" asked Roberta.

Blake glared at her. "Ma'am, if I told you what I really think of him, there wouldn't be another blade of grass in this valley for forty years."

Roberta rode alongside. "Do you really think you're justified in feeling that way about him?"

"Knowing what I do about him, ma'am, anything is justified."

She looked steadily at him, but she did not ask him to explain. Nor would he have offered an explanation. He was beginning to seethe with hatred of the man and his shrewdness. He had no use for Tinley the man and he didn't mind saying so, but to Roberta Blendick he wasn't going any further with it.

They traveled the meadow on the far side of the creek. About opposite the ranch-house, Red said, "These Star Under a Roof steers don't look too good, if you ask me."

"This must be the Indian cut," Blake said.

Roberta, now riding behind, said nothing. Docie, in the rear, kept urging the pack mule forward so he could hear what was said, but the pack mule was used to following Roberta's horse, and it refused to be hurried.

They were not bothered going down the valley. Blake opened the gate and they entered his own land. They rode straight through, and Mrs. White met them at the cabin. "What do you think is going to happen, Mr. Summers?"

"I don't know, ma'am. I hope it won't be too much."

"Chet was furious. He got all the homesteaders together and they rode to Mountain City. I'm afraid there will be violence, Mr. Summers."

"I'll try to stop violence, ma'am. I don't know what this man Tinley has got up his sleeve, and it is best to find out first."

"I pray you to use discretion."

"I'll use discretion, ma'am. You better pray that it works. For if it takes more than discretion, we'd best get it over with. I know this man, and I don't think he'll stop until he's ruined us."

"Tell Chet I don't want him to fight. Please tell him that."

"I'll tell him, ma'am, but he's a man," Blake said harshly. "I reckon the decision is up to him."

"Tell him I'll go over on Gunsmoke Creek if he wants to. Tell him I'll go anywhere!"

"I thought you liked it here."

"I do. Oh, I do." She began to sob.

Roberta moved up beside her. "It will turn out all right, Mrs. White. I'm sure it will. Mr. Summers will see to it."

"Docie," said Blake, "take your mother into the house."

Docie spoke up suddenly. "I'm going into town with you."

"You are like hell," Blake said brutally. "This is no place for kids."

"I can shoot straighter'n pa."

Blake touched the butt of his .44. "You want to start an argument now?"

Docie started, his mouth open. Then he swallowed. Something strange came on his face. Fear, perhaps; fear of a man he had trusted. He backed away, his face white.

Blake rode on. After a moment Red Flynn said, "What you tryin' to do — scare the kid out of a year's growth?"

"He's got his growth," Blake said, "and I don't want him to lose it. You know Tinley. He'd pick a target like that."

Roberta's shocked voice came out of the darkness behind him. "I don't think it is gentlemanly of you to say that Mr. Tinley would shoot children."

Blake shrugged. “Women and kids!”

Luke Leslie’s one-room cabin was dark. There was no light in the Crawfords’ place, and no lanterns around the barns. Ben Horton’s big place was dark too, but Mrs. Horton, mountainous in the dark, was sitting out in front in her special rocking chair.

“Hold up a minute,” she called.

Blake pulled his horse around. “Evening, Miz Horton.”

“Evening, Blake,” said the tired voice. “Goin’ for a ride?”

“Mountain City isn’t so far,” said Blake.

There was a rustle in the grass at Mrs. Horton’s side, and Blake made out the Shoshone girl.

“Depends on what you’re going in for,” said Mrs. Horton.

“It rightly does,” said Blake.

Mrs. Horton sighed. “Time was, before I had the fever and got my agy cake, that I could shoot as straight as Ben ever thought of shooting. I could draw as quick, too.”

“Gunfightin’s not a woman’s job,” said Blake.

“Ain’t it, though? Ask Ben sometime about them two rustlers I shot down in Nebraska.”

Blake swallowed. “Well, Miz Horton, maybe you been a gunfighter in your day, but I reckon you better sit this one out.”

“I’m sitting it out,” said Mrs. Horton. “Just do one thing for me, boy. If you throw down on Tinley, give him one just to the right of the breastbone, and then shoot his guts out.”

Blake heard a gasp behind him. Mrs. Horton chuckled. “Never had no use for smellin’-salts women.”

Blake grinned in the dark.

“Never had no use for Tinley, neither,” she went on. “Remember what I said. Do an artistic job. Don’t just kill him. Shoot up his carcass like a couple of Easterners runnin’ down antelope.”

“Well, it may be that we’ll get this settled without fightin’,” Blake said.

“Not unless you give the whole valley to Tinley. I seen this comin’ for a long time. We’re just lucky we had a man like you when it hit.”

Blake coughed. “We better get going. Where are your hired hands, Miz Horton?”

“They both went in to see the fight and help take care of Tinley.”

“I cannot understand,” Roberta said when they were out on the flat, “why everybody has it in for Mr. Tinley.”

Blake said grimly, “Maybe you *don’t* know it, ma’am — and maybe you don’t need to know it.”

She thought that over for a while. Red Flynn said suddenly, “Somebody’s coming behind us!”

“Move off the road,” said Blake.

He dismounted in the sagebrush, squatted down, and watched the skyline. The loping horse approached them rapidly. It came forward through the dark, and suddenly was past them, leaving a thick cloud of dust and the smell of bruised sage.

Blake straightened up. “Docie!” he called.

The rider brought the horse up on its haunches. "That you, Blake Summers?"

Blake got into his saddle. "This is me," he said, a little weary. "Where you going in such a hurry?"

"I was tryin' to catch up with you."

"How about your mother?"

"She's asleep."

"All right," said Blake. "You got a gun?"

"I've got dad's deer rifle."

"Got ammunition?"

"Yes, sir."

Blake sighed. "It's a good thing you aren't on the other side."

Docie's answer was breathless. "Yes, sir."

"Now, listen," said Blake. "You can go with us, but on one condition: you don't fire the first shot and you don't shoot at all until your dad or I either shoot or die. Got that?"

"Yes, sir."

"All right. See if you can hold that horse down to a trot the rest of the way. You don't want to walk into Mountain City, do you?"

"No, sir."

Roberta sounded perplexed. "Docie, I don't think you belong in this fight."

Docie said stubbornly, "Ma'am, I'm already in it."

They saw and heard the ruckus long before they pulled into Mountain City. From a distance, a confused rumble of voices rolled out over the sagebrush, with now and then a few words yelled in a louder voice but still not quite identifiable, though there was no doubt of the anger and pent-up feeling that impelled them.

The usual winking yellow lights from the hotel and the saloons, and the one over the watering trough, seemed for a time to show movement. Then Blake realized that there were other lights in Mountain City, and presently he saw that men were marching up and down the street carrying kerosene torches.

His lips tightened. He said aloud, “It’s a mob — and you can’t control a mob. They go crazy.”

Roberta’s voice came from his side, unexpectedly close. “They have an ugly sound,” she said. “It — it scares me.”

“It would scare anybody in his right mind. Come on, let’s get into town. And you, Docie, follow me — and keep your wits about you. Remember, no matter how much we hate Tinley, this is a country of law and order. If anybody kills anybody or destroys any property, the law will be here — and I don’t mean John Wall, either. Likewise, unless our hand is absolutely forced, we’ve got to take this on the chin and fight back through the courts. Otherwise we might as well give the country back to the Indians. You hear me, Bocie?”

A voice came from his left, a voice strong with new-found power and the quiet strength of maturity. “I hear you, Blake.”

Then Blake turned to the rear. “What do you say back there, Flynn?”

Red answered complacently. “I been sidin’ you ever since we was deputies for Billy Tilghman. I ain’t swappin’ horses now.”

"Deputies!" exclaimed Roberta. "I didn't kn—" Blake said briskly, "Let's get into town and break this up."

He jammed his spurs into the roan's flanks, and they lit out at a gallop. They pulled into the main street of Mountain City and met the mob in front of the bank. They were tramping up and down the dusty road, growling and muttering. Blake stopped before them on the roan. "What's got into you gents?"

"Tinley took our water," said a man in the back. "We're going to take Tinley."

Blake peered past the flickering yellow torches. "Who said that?"

The mob was suddenly quiet.

"You aren't ashamed, are you?" asked Blake. "You said it. Will you back it up?"

"Sure, he'll back it up!" two men said at once. "We'll all back it up."

"I'm not questioning your right to be mad," said Blake. "I'm mad myself. But I want to talk to you."

"We done too much talkin'," said another voice. "While we was talkin' and plantin' corn, J. J. Tinley was in Cheyenne gettin' a rail ready to ride us out on."

"Mebbe so," said Blake, "but this won't help. Who's that man who said he wanted Tinley?" He peered over the heads of the mob. "Will you come out here, mister?"

"I'll talk back here," the voice said.

"I like to see a man's face," Blake answered. "You aren't afraid to look me in the eye, are you?"

"Hell, no!" The voice was suddenly thick, and Blake knew the man was drunk. He turned to his rear. "Miss Roberta, this may get ugly. You better go home."

"I'm staying right here," she said firmly. "I want to see this through. There are a lot of things I don't understand about Mountain City, but I intend to learn."

"Your intentions are good," Blake told her, "but you're not staying here." He turned on her with what he hoped was a sneer. "D'you think I want to be handicapped with a helpless woman when I'm tryin' to fight down a riot?"

He looked around and saw the hesitation on her face, which was white in the torchlight. "Go look up Dr. Adams," he suggested. "We may need him."

He felt easier when he saw her swing the horse. Then he turned back to the man. A big, raw-boned fellow was pushing through.

"What's your name?" Blake asked.

Somebody shouted, "What's *yours?*"

Blake said in a loud voice, "That's a fair question. I'm Blake Summers and I bought out Potter, who had a homestead next to Washakie land."

"Whose side are you on?" asked the big man.

"You haven't told me your name," Blake reminded him.

"Art Powell."

"Where's your place, Art?"

"Over on Gunsmoke Creek."

"What are you doing in *this* mob, then? Gunsmoke Creek isn't affected by this order."

"It don't make no difference. If they can do it on Crazyman today, they can do it on Gunsmoke tomorrow."

"Sure, and they will too," said somebody else.

"Mebbe so, mebbe not."

"No *mebbe's* about it. It's already done — and damn' crooked politics. The state-house is *full* of crooks."

"I don't think it's that bad."

"Mebbe you ain't hurt," said a new voice.

Blake tried to look into the darkness past the torches. "I'm hurt first. What's the matter with you men, anyway?"

"We get a report today," Art Powell said, "and an eviction order tomorrow. Then what do we do? Are we just supposed to sit here and wait to be starved out?"

"We don't have to wait," Blake argued. "We can do something about it. There's plenty we can do, but for God's sake," he shouted, "let's find out for sure what we're up against before we go jumping off the deep end."

"Get down off your horse," a voice said from the back of the crowd. "Get down and let's see where you stand. Are you for us or with us?"

"I'm with you," said Blake, "but I'm not in favor of a mob." His voice rose. "You can't get a damn' thing accomplished this way. You go shoot up Tinley's office and maybe his place on Crazyman, and what happens? In a couple of days you've got U.S. marshals in here."

"We can lick any U.S. marshal that ever pulled a gun."

"All right, you whip the marshals and you've got a company of soldiers up from Cheyenne."

"Sure — paid by the same crooked politicians that took our water."

"Let's don't go calling names till we know where we stand."

He called louder. "Chet White, are you back there?"

"Show your face, Chet! We're not afraid of him."

There was movement in the crowd. Blake looked to his left. Red Flynn sat there, imperturbable but alert, his hands on his saddlehorn. Blake looked to his right. Docie had moved up to about three feet behind him. The boy's face was white, but he was steady as a rock. His rifle was in its boot. Blake faced front again as Chet White came out of the crowd. "Chet, what do you know about this?"

"I come to town right after you this morning," Chet said. His voice was a little thick, and Blake realized that he had been drinking. "The stage from Thermopolis had just come in, and I saw a Cheyenne paper in the post office. Somebody had pinned it up on the wall. It said the board of control had reclassified this water to a municipal use. That means Tinley's use."

Blake argued. "The town has got to have water, hasn't it? People have to live. And we need a town. If Mountain City wasn't here, we'd have to drive our beef to Thermopolis and we'd have to freight our supplies out of Thermopolis. That would take two days more each trip. Anyway," he added, "Mountain City can't use so much water. What they take isn't going to hurt us."

Chet looked up, his bony face filled with righteous indignation. He shook a long, loose forefinger at Blake. "The hell it can't!" he shouted. "You ain't read the paper yet! Go have a look. They reserved ten times as much water for Mountain City as the town needs. They stripped the valley clean. They took every acre-foot that comes down in the spring overflow! What do you think of that?"

Blake studied the man. A lot of things began to clear up. He asked, "What was the excuse for that?"

"To allow for the future growth of the town," Chet said. "That was the excuse but that wasn't the reason. The reason was to freeze us homesteaders out of Crazyman so J. J. Tinley can take over!"

CHAPTER FOURTEEN

Blake stared at Chet. "I hope you know what you're talking about," he said finally.

"It's still pinned up there in the post office. You can see for yourself."

Blake got down from his horse. The post office was half a block away. Together with Chet and Art Powell, whom Blake took along to avoid any precipitate action while he was gone, they went to the post office. On the wall next to the mail boxes, somebody had pinned up a single sheet, the front page of the *Cheyenne Tribune*, and with a pencil had drawn a circle around a small story. Chet held matches while Blake read slowly:

"The State Board of Control announced last week a reclassification of spring overflow water in Crazyman Valley, near Mountain City, from irrigation to municipal use, under the water act of 1890. Exact figures are not available, but it is believed this involves from 300 to 500 acre-feet of water. Clarence T. Johnston, State Engineer, said this was done to assure ample supplies of water for the growth of Mountain City, which had applied for a re-allocation of water to protect its probable growth."

Blake read it aloud. The last match died out, and Blake said in the dark, "The State Engineer can't possibly know what this means."

"Mebbe," said Art Powell, "but it's been done just the same."

"It's a big state," Blake said slowly. "He wouldn't know about every little valley and town, and the exact situation in them."

"It don't make no never-mind," said Chet. "It's been done and it leaves us settin' high and dry no matter *which* way you look at it."

Blake heard short, quick steps coming down the board sidewalk. Through the window he saw Red Flynn and Docie, sitting their horses like granite rocks in front of the crowd. The steps slowed down. A man came into the post office and went directly to a box. Chet White cleared his throat, and the man jumped. He was short and pudgy and wore a derby hat.

"Oh!" he said. "I didn't know there was anybody in here."

"We was readin' the paper, Mr. Rawson," said Chet.

Floyd Rawson bent back to his box. He struck a match and began to work the combination.

"You see this article in the paper?" asked Art Powell.

Rawson was counting to himself. "Three left — one, two, three, four, five — two right, back to — huh?" He stood up before he pulled the door open.

Blake was where he could see Rawson's face in the light from the torches out on the street. Rawson looked scared.

"You're Tinley's lawyer, ain't you?" asked Powell.

Rawson moistened his lips and swallowed. "I'm attorney for the Washakie Land & Cattle Company."

"You know about this water deal?"

"I'm sorry to say that's out of my jurisdiction."

Chet White got suddenly ugly. "How come it's out of your jurisdiction? You're also attorney for Mountain City, aren't you?"

"Well — yes, come to think of it, I am."

"Then how come you ain't been notified about this reclassification to municipal use?"

"I — well — I —"

"As city attorney, didn't you draw up the papers asking for this re-classification?" said Blake.

Rawson backed against the mail boxes. "Well, I hardly know how to answer that."

"You can answer it yes or no," Blake said.

"Well, yes." He looked from one face to another in the darkness. "That is — no. No, I didn't."

"Who did, then?"

"Why, I — the mayor, I suppose."

"How about the aldermen? Wouldn't they have anything to say about it?"

"I assume so."

"You assume too damn' much," said Blake. "You don't know who signed the application, do you?"

"I don't remember."

"In fact, you don't know if any formal application was made at all, do you?"

"I assume it was. It *must* have been."

"But you don't know."

"Not of my own knowledge — no."

Blake nodded. "About what we figured. You better get your mail and get out of here. And if you don't want your neck stretched, stay away from that mob."

"Yes, sir." Rawson was almost shivering as he fumbled with the box.

Rawson got his letters and a paper and scuttled out. Blake saw him going up the sidewalk away from the crowd. His steps came so rapidly it sounded almost as if he were running.

"Now," said Blake, "let's figure this thing out."

"They ain't nothin' to figger," said Powell.

"We know that Tinley did this by himself, without consulting the city government. Maybe it isn't even legal."

Chet snorted in the dark. "They've gone this far," he said. "They'll make damn' sure there's no loopholes. And if there was one, they'd plug it with money."

"That's right," said Powell. "The worst thing is — it's been done. The decision has been made and it will be hard to undo."

"We can appeal," said Blake.

"Sure. The courts can review a decision of the board — but how many times do they reverse one?"

"Not many," Blake said, "because most of the time the board is right. But when it's wrong, we can get it reversed."

Chet said, "You know how that goes. You'd spend years getting a decision reversed, and by that time we'd all be starved out. What are cattle going to do if there's no grass in the valley?"

"That's what I say," Powell maintained. "It don't do any good to be in the right if you get starved out doing it. I say let's go shoot up Tinley and clean out the Washakie ranch-house."

"You're crazy," Blake said harshly. "That won't change any legal facts — and that's all that counts. We could go shoot up the Washakie — and then what? Tinley would be sitting back laughing at us, because he'd still have the rights and he could slap damage suits on us for destruction of property and send some of us to the pen. That way he'd clean us out in a hurry."

Chet sounded ominous. "One thing sure. I don't aim to be cleaned out sittin' down."

"I thought you wanted to go over to Gunsmoke Creek."

"I wanted to go, all right, but I'm not going with a gun at my back."

"That's better than going with a hole in your guts."

"Mebbe you figger that way," said Chet. "I heard how you left Albany County. You was about to have a shootout with Tinley over some mavericks down there, and you got out. But I'll tell you this, Blake Summers: I'm no gunfighter, but I ain't afraid to stand up for my rights, neither."

Blake kept silent.

"When I saw you come into the valley," Chet said, "I told my wife, 'He looks like a fighter to me,' and the only thing I was scared of then was that you'd be too quick on the trigger and get us all in trouble. But I reckon I found out something else, Summers: you come here because you was yellow."

"He's right, ain't he?" Powell demanded.

Blake said slowly, "If I was afraid of Tinley, why would I come here in the first place?"

"I never been able to figure that out," said White, "unless you didn't know Tinley was up here."

Blake took a deep breath. Trust a man like this to figure out the answers when he got a couple of drinks in him.

"I'm fer goin' up the valley," said Powell, "and gettin' Tinley. When we stretch out his neck from his own wagon tongue, maybe he'll be reasonable."

"You'll never get a rope on Tinley's neck," Blake said suddenly. "When you go after him, you'll have to kill him or he'll kill you."

"Mebbe," Powell said slowly, "Chet is right. Maybe you *are* scared of Tinley. But I ain't!"

"Whether or not I'm afraid doesn't matter," said Blake. "I want you to know what you're facing when you crawl in a hole with Tinley. One of you is going to come out feet first."

"I'd rather have that," said Chet, "than have him take my land away from me. I worked hard for that land. I come in dog tired, along after the sun had set, an' I got up again before the sun was up. It ain't easy, makin' something out of a homestead, and it ain't easy to give it up. I say Tinley gets it over my dead body."

Blake hesitated. He had not realized the real depth of these men's hate for Tinley. Blake tried a new angle:

"Let's think this over. Suppose Mountain City *has* been awarded ten times as much water as it needs now, that isn't necessarily the end. The water has got to go somewhere, and it will keep on going where it has been going until Mountain City needs it. So nobody's really hurt — not right away, anyway. Why don't we all have a drink and go home? It'll look different in the morning."

Chet White didn't budge. "Mebbe you haven't heard the whole story yet."

Blake looked at the man's bony face in the dark. "If I haven't," he said slowly, "it's time somebody was telling me."

"It ain't complicated," said Chet. "Mountain City now has the right to all this flood water which it can't use, so until it gets ready to use it, the town has the right to lease it."

"To lease it?"

"You're mockin' me," Chet pointed out. "Yes, sir, they can dispose of it — and they already have."

Blake began to fish for makin's. He needed a drink.

"So Mountain City," Chet went on, "through its mayor, J. J. Tinley, has already leased its surplus water rights to the Washakie Land & Cattle Company. They're goin' to build a dam up in the mountains to impound the overflow of water and use it for its own benefit. And what will we get down in the valley when the spring thaw comes?"

"You said it." Art Powell sneered. "You get what the little boy shot at."

Blake shook his head. "You must be cr—" But he stopped suddenly. That very afternoon he had watched Roberta Blendick running contour lines on Poison Mountain. He had wondered what they were for. He had asked her, but she had not answered. Now he knew why. The valley — from Poison Mountain straight across to the other side — was narrow and deep and a natural place for a dam.

Art Powell said, “How do you feel now, Mr. Summers?”

Blake tried to control the ferocity that he felt in his brain. “I feel like talking to Tinley,” he said.

Chet White commented, “First sensible thing you’ve said.”

“There’s times,” Blake admitted modestly, “when I come up with a corker.”

CHAPTER FIFTEEN

But he didn't feel happy about it. What he had told them about Tinley was all wool and a yard wide: Tinley fought for keeps. If they cornered Tinley, somebody would die.

"Let's go out and talk to the crowd," Blake said.

They went outside. Red Flynn, still implacable, and Docie White, tall and somehow straighter, sat their horses before the mob. Blake's eyes narrowed as he saw that on each horse a rifle lay across the saddle.

Blake walked back and mounted the roan. "What do you say now, mister?" asked a voice.

Blake looked into the white faces before him. "There's no use hiding it," he said. "It doesn't look good."

The crowd burst into an explosive roar. "Let's get Tinley!" "We'll string 'im up!" "We'll show him who's running the country!"

Blake didn't move. He waited until they quieted down. "I'm going to talk to Tinley," he said. "I'll take one man with me."

"We'll all go!" they roared.

Blake leaned forward, his hands on the withers of the roan. "Is that fair — fifty to one?"

"It's fair with Tinley," somebody said.

"You don't mean that," said Blake. "You're men in this country, and you fight like men — even if you're fighting a skunk. I'll take one man with me — and you can choose him."

"Art Powell," said a voice.

"It would be better to have somebody from Crazyman," Blake suggested.

A man stepped forward, a rifle in his hands. "I'll go," he said.

Blake recognized one of the Crawfords — which one, he didn't know. They were all standing together and they all looked alike. Blake asked, "Does Crawford satisfy you?"

Chet White, obviously disappointed, said anyway, "I'll take Crawford."

Blake got down from the roan again. He put his hand on the neck of Red's dun mustang. "Can you hold 'em?"

Red said, "Long enough," and looked at Docie. "He's steady as a rock. I'm glad we brought him."

Blake turned to Crawford. "Come on — and don't fire the first shot. Back my play but don't shoot first."

Crawford nodded grimly and stepped out beside him.

Luke Leslie came out of the saloon and cut across the street. They met him in the middle.

"Can't figure out," said Leslie, "why you're workin' so hard to keep these gents from gettin' out of hand."

"Because it's right," said Blake.

"Isn't that John Wall's job?"

"It's anybody's job who believes in law and order."

"Where you goin' now, then?"

"To talk to Tinley."

"I'll go along."

"One's enough."

Luke Leslie growled. "A hundred isn't enough. You're a fool to go up there — the two of you. He'll have John Wall and half a dozen more."

"In that case," said Blake, "three aren't much better than two."

They left Leslie and got up on the opposite sidewalk.

"What do we say to Tinley?" asked Crawford.

"We say to him that if anybody is going to lease this water it's going to be us."

"You mean we'd have to pay for our own water."

"Until the case is settled in the courts. We could have the money put in escrow, and, if we win, we can divide it up among us according to what we paid."

"Did you say 'if we win'?"

They walked fifty feet on the boards. Finally Blake admitted, "There's no such thing as a cinch when you go to court."

"Unless you pay."

"I don't think that happens as often as it is said to. Every man who loses a case figures he was framed, but the courts generally try to be fair."

"If we lose this," said Crawford, "will you still say that?"

Damn the fellow! He hadn't said this many words in three years, but now — the worst of it was, Blake wasn't any more certain of justice than Crawford was.

Tinley was, as Perry Miller had said, a shrewd man. If there was a way of sewing it up legally, Tinley would do it. As a matter of fact, if there was such a way, you could be morally certain that Tinley had *already* done it. Blake felt grimmer as he walked toward the hotel. There would be no half-way with Tinley. It was just as Blake had told Chet White: if you called Tinley's hand, you'd better have good cards. He was a man who never bluffed because he never needed to. Tinley was a smart man, a mighty smart man. He looked a long way ahead and saw all the complications — and provided for them.

The thing was, Blake didn't want a mob doing it. A mob went crazy. It wrecked offices and burned buildings; it brought retribution upon itself and upon the family of every man involved. It was better for one man to do the job. If that man was clear-headed and stayed clear-headed, he could avoid a murder indictment.

"Stage is comin'," said Crawford.

Blake looked down the road. The big Concord was lurching over the ruts from Thermopolis, the six mules trotting, the driver's whip cracking. The Concord came out into the faint light from the torches, and the mules slowed down to a walk. The coach passed Blake and Crawford, and the driver called down, "Somebody's funeral?"

"Not yet," said Blake.

The coach went on around the corner. Blake and Crawford followed. The coach stopped in front of the hotel. A tall, gaunt man with long black mustaches and a soft black hat got down a little stiffly. He went directly across the board sidewalk and into the hotel.

A woman in a brown silk dress got off next. She was an unusually small woman, Blake noted, and the fact seemed to lodge in his brain somewhere, but he didn't know why. She turned back to the coach and helped four children to alight; the oldest was a girl about fourteen; the next two were girls, and the smallest was a boy. The driver held a well-worn cloth suitcase over the top, and Blake took it and set it down. The driver gave him a couple more, and Blake set them inside the door. The tall, gaunt man was talking to the room clerk.

The tiny woman in the brown dress thanked Blake, and went to the desk. Blake went back outside.

Luke Leslie met him, and said in an excited half-whisper: "Know who that is? That's Homer Mohr!"

Blake stared at him. "Who's he?"

"He's the man to see in Cheyenne if you want water rights."

Blake frowned. He said to Leslie, "Go on back and keep out of range."

He touched Crawford's arm and they moved up to the corner. The coach went by, headed for the livery to change teams. Blake and Crawford went around the corner.

The stairway to the office of the Washakie Land & Cattle Company was open and apparently unguarded. There was a light in the window upstairs, and a saddled horse at the foot of the stairway. Blake stepped forward to start up.

But a man stood suddenly in front of them. He was a short, heavy-set man with a big jaw, and he said, "What you want?"

"We come to talk to Tinley," said Blake.

John Wall said, "He's busy."

Blake said, "Aren't you marshal of Mountain City?"

"Sure."

"Then why aren't you out there taking care of that mob?"

"I'm busy," Wall said. "Get out."

"Maybe you don't hear so well," said Blake. "We came to see Tinley."

"Maybe you don't hear at all," said John Wall. "Mr. Tinley's busy."

Blake spread out a little from Crawford, so Wall would have trouble watching both of them. "Is Tinley upstairs?"

"Mr. Tinley's busy."

"Will you take a message to him?"

Wall didn't budge. The light upstairs went out. At the same time there was a movement from Wall, and he said, "Get back to the corner."

"But —"

"I'm holdin' a six-shooter on you," said Wall. "Don't make me use it."

Blake backed away.

"Turn around," Wall ordered.

Blake started the turn slowly. He meant to gain speed and wheel back on Wall to catch him off guard, ducking as he drew his own pistol. But Crawford was turning, too. Blake's shoulder struck the butt of Crawford's rifle and threw him off balance.

Heavy steps beat down the stairway, but Wall's pistol was in his back and Wall said in a low voice, "Keep your eyes straight ahead."

Blake heard the creak of saddle leather. Then a horse lunged forward, and its hooves beat out a hard gallop toward the sagebrush. Blake stood rigid, waiting for the pistol pressure to relax. The horse circled out in the dark somewhere, beyond sight even if Blake had been turned that way, and headed for Crazyman.

John Wall said, "Go on."

Blake shrugged. He said to Crawford, "He got away," and went around the corner to the front of the hotel.

The woman in the brown silk dress was talking to the clerk. Homer Mohr was pacing the lobby floor, smoking a cigar and giving an impression of impatience.

Blake stopped out in the dark and watched Mohr for a moment, trying to figure it out. Tinley had just taken their water rights away from them; Mohr was a man from Cheyenne. But Mohr was here — for what?

The answer suddenly became clear — just as Wall came around the corner from behind them. He passed them, walking rapidly, and went into the hotel carrying a Waldorf bag. He went up to Mohr and asked, "Where you from?"

"Cheyenne," said Mohr.

"Who you come to see?"

Mohr eyed the bag. "J. J. Tinley," he said.

Blake noticed the woman turned at the sound of the name, and moved toward them.

Wall started to hand the bag to Mohr, but Blake went through the door with long strides and said, "I'll take this."

The long fingers of his left hand closed on the grip. Wall glared at him, and Blake saw viciousness leap into the man's eyes.

They drew together. Wall's pistol was in a belt on the outside of his coat, but he never got it high enough. Blake's .44 bullet drilled him through the pit of the stomach, while Wall's bullet made a gouge in the inside calf of Blake's left leg.

Wall went down, trying to raise his gun, but Blake's pistol was centered on his forehead. Wall let the gun drop.

It was as well, for Wall was a dead man anyway. He began to vomit, and only then was Blake aware that the woman had screamed. The four children were huddled together, and one of the smaller girls was whimpering.

The lobby was filled with the acrid fumes of powder, and the smoke swirled against the yellow light of the oil lamp on the clerk's desk. Warm blood was running down Blake's leg and filling the bottom of his boot.

Mohr took hold of the bag. "This is mine," he said.

Blake still had his pistol in his right hand. "What's your proof?" he asked.

"Where's yours?"

Blake waved the .44 in a short arc. "I've got a writ of mandamus, or habeas corpus, or something or other right here that says you will have to prove ownership of this bag and what's in it before I give it to you."

"This man was handing it to me."

"You didn't have it yet," said Blake, "so as far as I'm concerned, it belonged to him. Therefore it's a part of the estate of a dead man and will have to be probated."

Mohr's jaws hardened and he turned white with fury, but he was an old man and there wasn't much he could do. He said finally, with iron in his voice, "I'm going to swear out a warrant for your arrest for the murder of this man. Murder and robbery."

"Do that," Blake said. "But get your hands off of this bag before I shoot you for attempted robbery."

Mohr turned loose slowly. He was furious but he was impotent. "You'll pay through the nose for this," he promised.

Dr. Adams hurried in, brisk and unruffled. "Where's the victim?" He saw John Wall on the floor, and went to him. He pulled down the man's shirt and looked at the bullet hole, a small dark spot in the man's skin.

The woman in the brown dress gathered her children on the other side of the lobby and tried to hide the scene from them.

Adams looked up. "You do this?" he asked Blake.

Blake nodded.

"Last time I saw," said Adams, "you were on the floor and Wall had the pistol."

Homer Mohr asked, "Will he die, doctor?"

Adams pulled back Wall's eyelids with the ball of his thumb. He watched the pupils closely. Finally he closed the man's eyes. "He's dead already," he said.

Mohr said, "I was a witness to this killing. Where can I find a justice of the peace? I want to make a statement."

"Ask for Bill Judson down at the second saloon. He's generally playing cards in the back there."

Mohr went out with long strides. Blake thought he knew what was eating on Mohr.

"You better stick around, son," said Adams. "Bill might decide to hold an inquest, and you might as well be here. You don't want to be indicted for murder, do you?"

"Not exactly."

"Of course I'm assuming it wasn't murder."

"Crawford was here. He saw everything."

Crawford nodded, but Adams shook his head. "This gent who just went out of here seemed to have more than a casual interest in this killing. You don't suppose he'd take the other side, do you?"

"I rather think he will."

"Then that's one against one," Adams noted. "Not very good odds when a man is charged with murder."

Blake frowned.

"Maybe the clerk saw what happened."

The clerk came across the floor. He was a man with thin, sandy hair and a hooked nose. "I'm sorry, gents. When the shooting happened, the lady was between me and it."

"The lady? Sure, she saw it all." Blake went over to the woman in the brown silk dress. "Ma'am, I'm sorry to bother you, but it might mean a lot to me to prove who drew first."

She stared at him, her brown eyes big. "I'm sorry," she said. "I was so frightened — I can't seem to remember anything that happened, except — there was fire and smoke, and I smelled gun-powder, and that man was lying on the floor, trying to raise his pistol." She shuddered.

Blake went back. Crawford was still standing at the door, holding the rifle. Adams had sat down. "Only thing I don't like," said Adams, "is the fact this fellow was town marshal, and also the fact he was present when you got gunwhipped last spring. Sometimes things like that influence a jury considerable."

Blake nodded slowly.

"I'd say," Adams went on, "it might depend a lot on what's in that bag."

Blake frowned. "How do you figure that?"

"That's Tinley's bag. I've seen it a hundred times. Everybody in Mountain City knows that bag. From which my guess is that John Wall was carrying it — Wall being a sort of handyman for Tinley — which also everybody knows. The thing that I don't know, and the thing a jury might like to know, is why you've got it now."

CHAPTER SIXTEEN

Blake looked down at the bag. He began to see what Adams was driving at. Then he remembered what Homer Mohr had said: "Murder and robbery." Mohr would not have said "robbery" in reference to an ordinary Waldorf bag. No, *Mohr knew what was in that bag!* That was why he became so furious when Blake took it.

"Here comes Perry," said Adams from his chair.

The little banker came in, his side whiskers more prominent than usual. He looked at Wall's body. "It seems we need a new marshal," he said presently.

Blake took the bag to Miller. "I took this from John Wall just before I shot him," he said, "or I just *started* to take it away from him when he pulled a gun on me."

Miller looked at him and pushed his derby back on his head. "What do you want me to do with it?"

"I want you to open it, in my presence and in the presence of Adams and Crawford, and see what is in it."

The banker eyed him for a moment. Then he took the bag and carried it over to the hotel desk. He set it up on top and began to work the catches. The top flew open. He looked inside and blinked his eyes, then looked again.

"Money?" asked Adams.

"How much is it?" asked Blake.

"This will take some counting," Miller answered.

He began to take out small rubber-banded stacks of yellowbacks and greenbacks. He laid ten stacks on the counter, and took out a canvas bag that clinked dully when he set it down. "Our sack," he remarked, pointing to the printed words, "Big Horn County Bank."

Blake waited. Miller began to count. Each bundle held a hundred bills. There were two bundles of tens, four bundles of twenties, and two bundles of fifties. "That makes twenty-two thousand dollars," said Miller.

"What's in the canvas bag?" asked Adams.

Miller poured out a double handful of gold coins and began to assort them. Presently he counted the coins in each stack and announced, "Exactly twenty-three thousand, all told."

"Put it back in there," said Blake, "and take it to your bank."

"I'll take it," said Miller, "but I'm not going to open the safe tonight. I don't like the looks of the mob outside."

"All I want," said Blake, "is to get rid of it — and for you to remember that I turned it over to you."

"Well, I won't forget that. Any time a man steps up to me in a hotel lobby and hands me twenty-three thousand dollars in cash, I figure my memory is good enough for that."

They watched him snap the bag shut. "Think you can make it to the bank?" asked Adams.

"I'm not taking it to the bank. I'm going to stash it somewhere else. I don't want my bank broken into."

"Want some help?"

Miller looked out the front door at the men. Still standing restlessly under the eyes of Red Flynn and Docie White. "Think I'll take a flyer out the back door — if one of you gents will cover me to see that I'm not waylaid back there." He grimaced. "Hate to be hit on the head and dumped into an old beer barrel."

Blake and Crawford went with him to the back door. There the banker disappeared in the darkness.

"Quiet," said Crawford.

"Yeah."

Wall's body was still on the floor when they got back. Blake's leg had begun to ache but it wasn't bleeding any more. His boot was full anyway, he figured, so it was just as well.

Adams picked up his black bag. "Your friend isn't back, so I don't suppose there will be an inquest tonight. Why was he so set on clearing John Wall's killing anyway?"

Crawford said nothing but stared at Adams.

The doctor turned. "Well, I'll get along. Somebody might take a notion to have a baby, night like this."

Blake watched him go. He was thinking about Mohr. Would the man testify against him at an inquest? He might, Blake realized, if he had had his heart set on that $23,000. A man might be real mad at having that much money jerked from under his nose.

And if Mohr testified against him, he had, as Adams had pointed out, only one witness for himself: Crawford.

It didn't look good to Blake. Crawford was an unknown quantity. You couldn't tell what he might do. Witnesses had been known to go to pieces and do some strange things under oath.

Following Crawford across the street, Blake began to see that he was in a mess. There seemed to be only one way out: to go catch Tinley and bring him back, put him and the lawyer up against each other and make them explain why John Wall was carrying $23,000 in currency.

By the time he mounted the roan, he knew that some way or other he had to get Tinley and bring him back. And that couldn't be done by assault. It would have to be by stealth. Two things Tinley didn't know: he didn't know John Wall was dead, and he didn't know that Perry Miller had the $23,000. Maybe those two facts could be used to advantage.

But how was he to get rid of the mob? He still had nothing to offer them, and pretty soon Crawford would tell them that Tinley had got away, and there'd be hell to pay.

He said to Red, "You got an extra .44 shell?"

"Sure."

"Who got shot?" a voice asked from the crowd.

Blake looked up. "John Wall," he said slowly, and punched out the empty case.

"Is he dead?" somebody asked.

"He's dead."

"What do we do now?"

"I think we all better hightail it home and get a good night's sleep. Tomorrow we'll come back in town and see what we can figure out."

He sensed that the temper of the crowd was dropping.

Out on the edges, two or three turned hesitantly toward the saloon. One man walked across the street and got his horse. Blake began to hunt for makin's.

Then he heard a hard-galloping horse come across the sagebrush, and a high-pitched woman's voice: "*Coon'-ah!*" Blake looked up. That was the Shoshone word for fire.

The crowd moved like one person. They turned to watch Soft Hands slide from the barebacked horse and run to Blake Summers. "The men are burn all the houses!"

Old man Horton charged through the crowd and grasped her fiercely by the shoulder. "They burned my house?" he roared.

She hunched down as if she feared that he would strike her. "*O'*-se."

"Where's my wife?" demanded Horton.

"I took her — in the hills," said Soft Hands.

The crowd was a mob again. They turned together like steers frightened by a wolf howl, and they stampeded like a herd, all headed in one direction in the same instant and without thought. They started running, most of them on foot. Red looked at Blake. Docie waited.

"It looks to me," Blake said, "like Tinley has just thrown away a royal flush."

Chet White came up, pale with fear. "What about my wife?" he asked.

Blake said, "Red, you and Docie get in the lead. Don't let these gents do anything crazy if you can help it."

"There's no use dodgin' it," said Red. "There's a full blown range war comin' on tonight. You might as well sail into it with your guns loaded."

"I'll sail. You light out and keep the leaders in sight."

The Crawfords were already galloping into the sagebrush. Blake got off of his horse. "Look here, Soft Hands. Did you see who was in the bunch that burned the ranch-house tonight?"

"I not know them all," she said. "Mister Stewart with green vest and the Mexican, Tomás — them I know."

"You're sure of that?"

Her eyes were wide. "*O'-se.*"

"All right. I'll take you over to the hotel and get them to put you up for tonight, and when morning comes we'll figure out what to do next."

"I maybe go back to reservation," she said. "One man up there has ask me to live in his teepee."

"That might not be the worst deal in the world," said Blake, while at the same time he half envied the man. She sure was an armful; no doubt of that. He went across the street with her and walked into the lobby. Blake went to the desk. "Have you got a —"

He heard a little scream behind him, and turned around to see the Shoshone girl fall on the dead body of John Wall.

Blake said slowly, "Well, I'll be damned!" He turned to the clerk. "When she gets through weepin', put her up for the night and I'll pay for it."

"Was she you squaw?"

"I don't know that she was anybody's squaw. From the way it looks, she must have been promised to John Wall. And from the way it sounds, she's tryin' to wake him up."

"I can't have that going on all night."

"Then get rid of the dead man," said Blake.

"I don't dare touch him till the J.P. gets here."

"Well?"

The clerk shrugged and went back behind the desk. Blake took a look at Soft Hands, howling with grief over John Wall, and went outside. He mounted the roan at the watering trough and rode across the sagebrush at a lope.

He saw now the glowing ruins of Horton's big house. Horton and his two men were out in front, fogging it across the sagebrush. By the time they reached the house they'd be afoot. Chet White was right behind them, riding in desperation, for he was hanging onto the saddle-horn with both hands.

Blake wasn't worried too much about Chet's wife; he didn't think Cotton Stewart would let his men hurt her. Chet's wife might be afoot, and she might be scared to death, but she probably wouldn't be hurt.

What Blake was trying to figure out was why Tinley had done this. The man had had everything his own way; he'd taken over their water; he was running things to suit himself, and Blake knew that the chance of homesteaders' reversing a decision of the board of control was slim. Tinley knew that as well as Blake did; why, then, had he pulled this bonehead?

Looking at it another way, Tinley had prepared this at least early in the day, for he hadn't had time to ride up to the Washakie ranch-house and bring back his crew of gunslicks. No, Tinley would just about now be entering his own land.

There was one explanation: the man's incredible hostility toward homesteaders and small ranchers. No, deeper than that; his monstrous egotism. It wasn't enough to run the homesteaders off by taking their water. It wasn't spectacular enough for Tinley. The water rights affair was the surest way there was to get rid of them, and Tinley knew that — but he had to have one last splurge of gloating. There was no other way to explain a man like Tinley. It wasn't winning that he liked as much as it was grinding under his heel the little men whom he hated — probably because he himself had been a little man once.

Blake sighed. It wasn't sense that started range wars. A man got too big for his britches. If it wasn't for that, a lot of range wars could have been avoided. But in the beginning the cattle kings were insulted because their supremacy was disputed, and a man insulted is a dangerous man. Every day in the early west, men walked straight into death with blazing guns for that very reason. They could be pushed so far and no further. They stopped and fought although they knew they would die for it.

This was something of the same thing, but distorted. The plain truth was that Tinley couldn't be happy over just winning the land; he wanted to see the homesteaders squirm.

Horton and his men had split, riding around the glowing embers of his big house and all that had been in it. The barn was a bed of glowing ashes, and the corn from which Soft Hands had fed the chickens was a smouldering bank of fire. The corrals were a ring of slowly burning fence posts, for cottonwood didn't burn too freely. The harness shed and two wagons were in ashes, and old man Horton was cursing steadily. Blake didn't blame him.

Chet White was beating his horse on up the road. Blake called to him, and finally went after him and held him back. "Don't kill a good horse," he said. "She'll be all right. They wouldn't hurt a woman."

Chet almost sobbed. "The dirty yellow coyotes!"

"Take it easy," Blake said. "She'll hear us, and she'll come to meet you."

Even Horton's outhouse had been burned to the ground, and Horton began to ride in circles toward the hills, calling: "Jes-sie! Jes-sie!"

Chet was going up the road at a walk now, and Blake glanced behind him. There were about thirty men there, and most of them were watching Horton, but Blake had no illusions as to what was in their minds or would be in their minds when they once got started up the valley.

He thought to look ahead. The Crawford cabin had burned down and was nothing but glowing ashes; their outbuildings were flat too. Leslie's place was still burning in one corner, and it was plain that they had fired his corn, for the entire twelve acres looked like thick brush just after a forest fire had gone through — embers everywhere, and occasionally a little piece of dry leaf would burst into flame, blaze up, and die down.

Chet White's place was still burning at a good clip.

Blake looked on up the valley to his own place, three miles away. The cabin that he and Docie had built that summer was blazing fiercely. His corrals were going up in rings of fire; his wagon was burning, and the small shed where he had planned to store his feed was falling in.

Horton had found his wife and jumped off of his horse to help her. The mob was beginning to mutter — and now it was such that Blake could do nothing. You couldn't argue sense into men who were watching every penny of their property except livestock go up in smoke. You couldn't temporize; he knew that. Soon now these men would want to kill.

He saw Docie trotting toward his father. He called the boy. "Tell Red to hold them back as much as he can. I'll go with your father. And don't worry about your mother. I don't think they'd dare to touch her."

Docie wheeled his horse and went back to Red Flynn. Blake took out after Chet. He heard the mob raise shouts when Mrs. Horton came into view, and he wondered what Tinley would have done if Mrs. Horton had been burned to death. Probably he figured the Shoshone girl would take care of her, and planned the fire that way. It was risky, but that was like Tinley.

He caught up with Chet as they passed the Crawford place. They rode on past Luke Leslie's burned-out corn field. They reached Chet's place. "You go around one side," said Blake, "and I'll go around the other."

Chet rode around the right, calling "Liz!" in a voice that started strong but faded out when it got in the upper register. Blake put in his two cents' worth, calling, "Lizzie White!"

Then he heard a sound like Chet choking, and saw the woman coming to him over the grass. She fell before she got there, and Chet jumped down and picked her up, swinging her back and forth in his arms like a baby.

Half an hour later the rest of the men were standing by as Blake rode around the ashes of his own place. A terrible hardness was rising in him, but he put it down. He remembered that he had to bring Tinley back alive — and he told himself he must not forget that. But he didn't know how. The men were here. He hesitated now to call them a mob. They were after blood and they were deadly, not crazy.

Art Powell rode up, stone sober. "We're goin' up there after Tinley," he said. "We voted to have you lead us. If you don't want to go — all right, you don't have to. But if you say you'll lead us, we want some action. No more talk. There's been too much talk. We're goin' after Tinley, and we're goin' to bring him back, dead or alive, along with Cotton Stewart and his whole gang of gunfighters. Like I say, we voted to ask you to lead us. Do you want it?"

Blake looked up at him. He looked at the men behind him — a mass of white, deadly faces. There were only two ways out. These men could ride up there on their own, and probably all get ambushed and killed, or he could lead them and save as many as possible. It wasn't much of a choice. He looked back at the glowing ashes of his cabin, then at the men, and said, "I'll lead if you'll do what I say."

CHAPTER SEVENTEEN

Blake went into conference with Art Powell and with Luke Leslie, who had worked around the Washakie ranch-house for a few months before he homesteaded. The rest of the men rode out through the meadow, catching up horses. Red Flynn and Docie pulled up and sat in on the conference.

"If they're holed up in the big house," said Leslie, "it'd be plain suicide to rush 'em. Them logs are fourteen-inchers."

"It's within gunshot of the yellow rocks on the west and north," Red Flynn noted.

"That it is. A man could sit up there all day, pickin' them off."

"How about water?" asked Blake.

"The well is out by the harness shed, about a hundred feet from the house."

"And food?"

"That's in the cellar — and there's always enough to last a month. Cotton Stewart likes to eat."

"How far would you say the rocks are from the ranch-house?"

"Maybe two hundred yards at the closest point."

"Too far," Blake said, "to shoot burning arrows."

"Pretty far."

"But not too far for a good man with a Winchester."

"At two hundred yards," said Art Powell, "shootin' from a rest, I'll guarantee to drill a man between the eyes."

"We can starve 'em out, then," said Red.

"I don't think so," said Blake. "Here's the trouble. This thing has developed into a war. Ev'rybody in Mountain City knows about it, and it's only a question of time — and not much time — until the governor will send troops in here to chase us out."

"Him not being exactly a friend of the little man," Art Powell said.

"He'd have to do it no matter who was involved. You can't have an armed insurrection in any state. So we've got to clean this thing up fast."

Docie was watching him with open mouth. Red Flynn was listening for orders. Chet White came up with Ben Horton. They were now, Blake figured, a good forty strong.

"I got an idea," said Blake. "First off, we'll all go riding up the valley whoopin' and hollerin' and firin' a few shots."

"So they'll know exactly where we are." Art Powell sounded disappointed.

"Sure enough. They'll figger we're comin' in for a head-on attack, and they'll pull back into the ranch-house and the buildings and around the corrals. We ride up close but not close enough to get within gunshot. Then we circle around a little, makin' a lot of noise but not doin' any damage."

"The hell with that," Art Powell said explosively. "I want to do some damage."

"You said you would do what I said," Blake reminded him.

"All right. I said it and I'll do it, but I want action."

"Good. Now, while we're ridin' up toward the ranch-house in a body, Red and Docie and say three others with rifles will climb up the rocks on the blind side and get located in a protected spot about a hundred feet up, where they can see the whole layout."

"And keep 'em pinned down in the house," said Red.

"That's it. Run 'em in the house and keep 'em there. But don't forget," Blake told Red, "to be sure you've got a way out — just in case. You don't want to be caught like steers up against a bobwire fence in a blizzard."

"I'll watch that," said Red.

"All right. Go pick your men and get ready to travel. But don't leave until we get a quarter of a mile ahead."

"You named your poison," said Red, and rode off toward the big group, followed by Docie.

"You all set, Docie?" asked Blake.

Docie reined back. "I don't know if I've got enough shells," he said.

Blake chuckled. "That's what I thought you'd say. Borrow some from the bunch that's going with me."

"Now," Blake told Powell and Chet and Horton, "after we raise a little ruckus out of gunshot for a couple of hours, it'll be gettin' along toward daybreak. We'll pull back toward the creek."

"I don't like retreatin'," Powell said.

"We pull back to the creek, fire a few shots, and then cross the creek up into the hills on the other side."

"They'll think we're crazy."

"Not so crazy. That sun will be hot out there along the creek, and there isn't enough shade for all of us. We'll be stashed in the hills and we can drop a few long shots when they come for water, but the real pressure will be from Flynn's boys. They'll be close enough to give plenty of trouble to anybody who goes for water. A few will get through, but remember: there's forty or fifty men holed up in that place. A gallon or two of water won't go very far. And what about the horses? They'll be putting up a fuss."

"What good will it do to make a horse thirsty?" asked Powell.

"There are men," said Blake, "who can't stand to hear an animal suffering for water."

Chet White nodded against the stars. "That's a smart idea."

"So along about the time it gets dark tomorrow, these gunhands are going to be tired of being sniped at from the rocks. They may be a little thirsty themselves, and some of them will be walking the floor listening to those horses neigh and watching them paw the ground."

Horton said slowly, "So they'll figure on makin' a rush for the creek as soon as it gets dark."

Blake said, "That's the way I figure it. In the meantime, we'll drift down from the hills as soon as it gets dark, and we'll be waiting for them."

"It'll be a massacre!" Powell shouted.

"There's only one thing — I want Tinley alive."

Nobody answered for a moment. Then Powell said, "You told us yourself, up there in Mountain City, that Tinley would never be taken alive. You said somebody would have to die when he got cornered."

"I figger that's right," said Chet.

"Me too," said Horton.

Blake didn't answer for a moment. Finally he faced it. He had spoken the truth, and they were right: there was no more hope of taking Tinley alive than there was of sneaking up on a coyote in the dark. He let out his breath in a rush. "We'll take him dead, then." He didn't have time to figure a way out. One thing was sure: there'd be grand juries in Big Horn County for years after this affair, and they'd all be in hot water. "You fellows get over there with the bunch. Each pick about a third of the men, and each be responsible for what those men do. We've got to do what I said. If we don't do it right, those boys up on the yellow rocks may be cornered like rats."

"I thought you told 'em to find a way out," said Powell.

Blake turned on him scornfully. "You know damn' well there's no way out if a couple men get above them on the hill. It's up to us to keep that from happening."

Powell shut up. The three men moved off to the main body and began to choose their squads.

"Send an extra man along with Flynn for a messenger," Blake said, "and leave a couple for me."

Luke Leslie said admiringly, "You sound like a colonel."

The three leaders got their squads lined up. Red Flynn and his men were ready. Blake rode out before them. "Now, remember, we aren't going to attack tonight. We're just attracting attention. Don't get within rifle range. We don't want anybody hurt. And when I give the word, work your way back to the hills across the creek. Everybody got that?"

"We got it."

"Who's comin'?" asked Chet.

Blake listened. "Somebody's foggin' up the road from town," Horton observed.

"Let's move on," said Powell.

"We better see what this is."

"It might be the sheriff."

"How could the sheriff get here so quick from Basin?"

"He could of come up from Thermopolis."

"What's the difference where he came from?" Chet argued. "If he's after us, he'll get us. We might as well wait and see."

The horse was galloping hard. Blake rode out to meet it. "Ho! What's the rush?"

"Blake Summers!" said a woman's voice. "I knew I'd find you up here."

He touched the brim of his hat. "I take it that's a compliment, ma'am."

"Definitely not." Roberta Blendick sounded positive. "I had hoped better from you than the head of a band of murderers and looters."

"Well, now, ma'am, seems to me you're a little hasty with words like that. Do you know who burned every building in this valley and who turned loose every horse? Do you know who set every woman in the valley afoot?"

For a moment she didn't answer.

"The men are in a bad mood, ma'am," said Blake. "You can't go around burning people's homes and chousing up their families and expect a man to turn the other cheek."

"There's the law," she said.

"I been all over that," Blake told her. "I know both sides of the argument. I know that when a dog goes mad you don't wait for the law to come and shoot it. A man has got the right to defend himself."

"You aren't defending yourself now. You're making a deliberate attack."

"Deliberate but not unprovoked, ma'am. There's such a thing in the law as provocation. Some things make a man pretty mad. Do you see those ashes over there, still burning? Yesterday," he said, "that was my house. Those were my corrals."

"You could sue."

He really laughed then — a bitter laugh. "Me — a homesteader — sue a man like Tinley — in this state where the big cattleman has always been a king?"

"You could get a verdict."

"Yes, ma'am, I might. I might spend years of time and thousands of dollars, and I might get a verdict — and by that time I could be starved out a dozen times over."

"But this isn't pay for damages you're after," she argued. "It's for nothing but revenge."

At last he saw it clearly, for the first time this long night, and he was grateful to Roberta Blendick for making him see it. "No, ma'am, it isn't that exactly. It's a way of settling the Crazyman question once and for all, of showing Tinley and other big cattlemen that the little man has a right to live, too."

"What will you do if you get him?"

"If we get him, we'll take him to Thermopolis and put him in jail for trial for arson and conspiracy to arson. If we take him dead, we'll send his carcass back to his family in Albany County."

He knew she winced, but he was past caring. She said once more, "You're burned out. Can you get the money to rebuild?"

"Maybe not," he admitted.

"Then" — he sensed that she was close to tears — "what's the object in all this fighting and killing?"

"Ma'am," said Blake, "it's always been like this. Some men come along and they do the fighting. Some of them die, and those who live seldom get any benefit out of it. But there are people who come after, ma'am — farmers, ranchers, carpenters, lawyers, school teachers, editors, druggists, and bookkeepers. They can come and they can stay in safety, because others have been before them and have made it safe for them."

"Is it worth dying," she asked in a low voice, "to clear the way for somebody else?"

"Maybe it is," he said, "maybe it isn't." The roan moved, and he found his arm around Roberta. "Is it worth living," he asked, "to know you haven't got the courage to do anything but run?"

Her head was against his chest and she was weeping silently; her tears fell on his forearm. He pulled her close to him, and her arms went around his neck.

"Blake!" she whispered. "I don't want you to be killed."

He was suddenly filled with vitality and assurance. "I'm not aiming to be, ma'am — not now."

"You've been on both sides of the fence tonight," she said finally. "Don't you know what you want to do?"

And at last he did know. He knew now beyond any doubt why he had left Albany County — he had not wanted to kill. To himself he had made the excuse of not wanting to leave four children without a father, and some, like Red Flynn, had wondered about that.

Those doubts didn't bother Blake any longer. He knew he had not been running away back in Albany County, for he was in the same situation now and he wasn't running. Having an army behind him didn't make any difference, for he knew Tinley and he knew that at the end somebody would have to go in after him, like pulling a lobo wolf out of a cave. If he had done it years ago he would have saved this mess tonight, but he hadn't done it then, so he would have to now. And he wasn't fighting himself in his mind any more. He was going after Tinley and that was all there was to it.

The men were talking together impatiently and he released her. "You better ride back down to the old Horton place," he said. "Miz White and Miz Horton are there."

"You ready now?" Art Powell called.

Blake watched Roberta turn her horse and start back down the valley. He rode up to Horton's squad and said, "I'm ready. Make all the noise you want, but stay out of gunshot."

They moved off. For a little while the men were silent. They had begun to realize this was a thing that would mean funerals for some of them. A sagehen whirred off to the right, and Blake knew that Red Flynn and his party were headed for the rocks.

Horton said, "I thought for a minute that was Soft Hands."

"You mean the Shoshone girl?"

"Yeah, the one that worked for me."

Blake was puzzled. "What would she be doing up here this time of night?"

"Ridin' up to see a friend, maybe."

"A friend? What are you talking about?"

"She come from the reservation, and she never even had no Indian upbringin'. Her parents was killed by white goldminers and she was taken over by an older halfbreed." Horton paused. "I reckon it warn't long before she learned one way a woman can get what she wants."

"But she never married."

"Nope. Don't know why that was. John Wall practically beat her to make her marry him, half a dozen times."

Blake nodded as they jogged along. "That makes sense. She fell on Wall's body up there in the hotel and went into the death chant."

He heard Horton take a deep breath. "I reckon she's a woman capable of lovin' a lot of men. I heard of women like that."

"What are you driving at?" asked Blake.

Horton drawled, "That Shoshone girl has been Tinley's mistress for three years."

CHAPTER EIGHTEEN

They rounded the big chimney of yellow rock and broke into wild yells. Two or three pistol shots were fired.

The ranch-house was dark, and Blake knew he had guessed right. Cotton Stewart had drawn his forces inside, awaiting the assault. Tinley would be there, too.

They rode back and forth in front of the big building, and around the sides, but not near the corrals. A few shots were fired at the building, and at first there was no reply, but presently an answering shot came in the shape of a blast of red and yellow fire. Blake watched carefully. Somebody inside had disobeyed orders. Tinley would be drinking bourbon and swearing.

Blake watched the sky over the mountains to the east. At the first sign of lightening he called off the men, and they drew back toward the creek.

"Tinley will figure we were afraid to attack him," he told them.

"It wouldn't look right to me," said Art Powell.

"Besides," said Horton, "it ain't what Tinley would do himself. How do you figure it?"

"I'm figuring it the way Tinley figures it. Sure, Tinley would find a way to attack, but Tinley thinks Tinley is the only great man in the world. It doesn't occur to him that somebody else might do what he does. He doesn't expect them to. He expects other men to play the coward."

Chet White said dubiously, "Maybe you're right."

"I know Tinley."

They took up positions along the creek and exchanged a few shots. Presently Blake, watching from a willow tree upstream, saw a booted man in a tall hat, carrying an empty bucket, warily leave the back door of the building and start for the pump. Suddenly his hat seemed to be jerked off. Then the sound of a shot floated down from the rocks. Blake looked up. A small puff of smoke hung over a crevice lined with bushes.

The man grabbed his hat. Another shot sounded. The man dropped the bucket and ran back into the house. The bucket jumped, and a third shot floated down. Blake grinned. Trust that Red. He had put a hole through the bucket to give them warning.

The next man out tried to run, but the bullets from above kicked up small gouts of dirt around his feet. He got to the pump, turned his back to the rocks and began to work the handle. Then he fell over the handle, and another shot came down; Red was through playing. The man gradually slid off the pump handle and rolled over on his back, one arm outstretched.

Then Tinley's men tried to concentrate their fire on the rocks while two more men went for water, but, at Blake's signal, his men began to pour lead through the windows of the ranch-house. In a moment there was an answering fire from inside. Blake signaled his men to keep shooting. The two men picked up the dead man and started back to the house. One of them stumbled, coughed blood, and fell over the dead man's legs. The third man hesitated, then ran for the house.

There were two dead men on the ground now. There would be forty or fifty more men inside that house. That many men could want an awful lot of water.

The sun came over the mountains and began to burn down in the valley.

"We've got the weather with us," said Chet White. "There ain't a breath of air stirrin'."

Blake asked for a three-man detail from each group.

"Three of you," he said, "go downstream a way — not out of sight of the ranch-house — to keep tab on who tries to come upstream."

"And stop 'em?" asked a tall farmer in overalls.

"Well, as long as we're having a war, I reckon we can't let just anybody go in there."

"That's what I wanted to hear."

"Three of you go up the valley to a point where you can command the road. If one or two come down, stop them. If there should be a good sized party, fire a few shots to scatter them and signal us." He turned to the first three. "That goes for you too."

"What if it's the law?"

"If it's really the law, you better let 'em go where they want to go."

Art Powell growled, "There's two dead men out there in the back yard now. I don't see no reason for playin' patty-cake with the law."

Blake shrugged.

He saw the two parties leave, one upstream, one down. "Now," he said to the other three men, "get good positions on the creek and keep the boys occupied in the house. The rest of us will go back up to the hills."

"What's that for?" asked Horton.

"For one thing, it'll make them think we've got twice as many men as we have. And scared men get panicky and hard to handle."

"But why would any of us be going to the hills anyway?"

"To get out from under fire and get some rest for tonight. Don't you figure tonight would be the logical time for us to take a crack at them?"

"I reckon."

"All right, come on now; straggle up there, as if it was every man for himself."

"All right, general," said Art Powell.

Blake sent two more men to butcher one of his yearling steers. They built a fire back in the rocks, while two men went into Mountain City for bread and coffee.

"Big ruckus going on in Mountain City," they reported later. "Everybody's talkin' about the range war."

"But nobody's doing anything?" asked Blake.

"Not when we left. There was talk of wiring the governor, but everybody has so little use for Tinley that nobody wants to spend money on a wire."

"How about the sheriff?"

"He hasn't showed up. Maybe he figured this was a good time to go lookin' for horse thieves."

Blake breathed easier. If they could get by until tonight without interference from the law, he thought he could settle this for good.

All morning long there was desultory firing, with nobody hurt. But Red Flynn's party kept the gunfighters pinned down in the ranch-house. They made two attempts to bring in the bodies, but Red drove them back, and presently a buzzard settled down. There was a shout from inside the cabin and a shot. The buzzard crawled off a few feet and died.

A little after the sun was directly overhead, Blake rode down to the creek with sandwiches for the three sharp-shooters.

"Got plenty of ammunition?" he asked.

"Plenty. We ain't hittin' anything, though."

"It isn't necessary," said Blake. "You can win a war without hitting a man."

"What do we do tonight?"

"Stay right here in the shade until they bust out of the house to attack. That'll be after dark, I think. If it isn't, we'll cover you from the hills. When the attack comes, you three run."

"Then they'll get to the water."

"That isn't the end of the story," said Blake. "They'll also find themselves between two fires."

"Good enough."

The horses in the corrals back of the ranch-house began to neigh for water. After an hour of this, the back door was flung open and Cotton Stewart ran out to the corral. Bullets spattered around him, but he reached the corral gate. He turned to face the yellow rocks and shook his big fist. "Go to hell, you —"

He stopped talking suddenly, a leg doubled up under him. He lay there for an hour in the hot sun, alternately trying to reach the corral to release the thirsty horses, who now were pawing the fence, and trying to make headway toward the ranch-house. But Red held his fire.

Presently Tomás ran out, hurling a stream of Spanish blasphemy. He dragged Cotton back in the house and was unmolested. Then he ran out, no doubt at Tinley's urging, and started to open the corral gate. A bullet caught him in the side, and he rolled over and over. "Santa María! Santa María!" he cried, and his high voice carried across the valley.

Blake Summers watched without expression, but not quite without feeling. It was a costly thing, a war like this, but the worst of it was, the one responsible wouldn't be the one to pay the most.

Blake saw a man crawling down the far side of the yellow rocks, and sent a man to meet him with meat and bread. The man took the food and four canteens of water and went back up the rocks.

The thirsty horses' neighing now was pitiful. Blake watched with narrowed eyes. He'd seen horses go for three days on the desert, carrying a load, without a drop of water, but these brutes, penned up and with nothing to do but want water, were putting up an awful fuss.

About mid-afternoon there was a ruckus from the down-stream guards. Blake had watched a lone horseman approach for a couple of miles, but the guards stopped him, and Blake went down.

One of the guards, holding the rider's hands twisted behind him, grinned over his shoulder at Blake. "We sure got one here."

Blake swallowed hard and said to Soft Hands, "What are you doing here?"

"I am going to Mister Tinley."

"What for?"

"I think he want me to."

Blake asked suspiciously, "You bringing any message from anybody?"

"Me?" She showed white teeth. "No. Course not. I not see anybody."

Blake began to fish for makin's, thinking hard, remembering what Horton had said. "I thought you were in love with John Wall," he said. "That was a pretty good act you put on up there in the hotel."

She said calmly, "I have love John Wall. But he is dead."

Blake studied her. Yes, John Wall was dead — and Horton had said she was a woman who could love many men. So now she was going to Tinley. "You sure didn't waste any time," he said.

"Mister Tinley always say he want me. I go to him now."

He thought about it. With Soft Hands in the ranch-house, the crows would start swarming. And Tinley — what would he do?

Blake nodded. "Go ahead," he said. "But you better carry a white flag so they won't shoot at you."

"I have nothing," she said, wide-eyed, "but my dress and moccasins."

"Here." Blake tore a piece out of his shirt-tail and tied it on a stick.

She took it, and regarded him gravely. "I thought sometime," she said, "I would come up and keep your cabin for you. But you never ask me."

Blake stared at her, at the depths of her black eyes, and knew she meant it. "You better get going," he said roughly.

Then he mounted the roan and rode back up to the hills.

"What you doin'?" asked Chet White. "Makin' things comfortable for Tinley?"

"I doubt it," Blake said. "I doubt it very much."

"If you're figurin' they'll fight over her — remember, Tinley's still boss of the Washakie."

"I'm not sure of that," Blake said softly. "Tinley hired a rough crew. They know they were burning and looting illegally last night, and they've been pinned down all day without water, and with men shooting at them whenever they show hide." He watched Soft Hands ride up to the house, dismount, and walk across the porch. The door opened cautiously, and she slid inside.

During this time the men at the creek had held their fire. Now, as the door closed, a shot sounded, and the porcelain doorknob dissolved into white dust.

"Nice shootin'," Blake observed.

"The best," said Art Powell.

Blake looked at the sun, at the men scattered through the rocks, making coffee, eating bread and meat, checking their weapons.

"I want six men," Blake said. "Six good men who can move quietly."

One of the Crawfords came forward, and two younger men whom Blake didn't know. "Take Stark over there," said Powell. "He can whip his weight in wildcats and he moves like a snake." He grinned. "I can fight, but I'm sure clumsy when I start bein' careful." Stark was a tall, thin man who wasted no words; he picked up his rifle and came forward. "Two more," said Blake, and Powell went looking among the rocks. He came back grinning. "Here they are — the Notting brothers. They'll do your job."

Blake looked around him. "That leaves about twenty-two here in the hills, if I've counted right. I want you fellows to stay up here and cover those three men down by the creek. Send word to the guards upstream and downstream that we're looking for action after dark, and that they're not to bite off more than they can chew."

"Who's in charge here?" asked Art Powell.

Blake looked at him. "You are — but do exactly what I tell you."

Art grinned.

"Keep your men right here to cover those three down at the creek. You can spread out a little just outside of the hills about dark, but don't go down to the creek. When the rush comes from the ranch-house, all I want you to do is keep 'em busy."

"Where'll you be?"

"I'll be in hot water if you don't do what I say."

Blake said to his six men, "Get your horses." He led them a little higher into the hills, then turned northeast. They traveled downstream, parallel with the creek, for a mile, and Blake led them into the meadow and across the creek. They watered their horses and went up the other side. They had crossed below the guard, and Blake had waved them back when they started down to inquire. Under cover of the yellow rock lookout where Red Flynn was posted, they got into the hills and upon the slope of Poison Mountain. By this time the sun was hidden, and the southeastern slope of the mountain was in shadow. Blake worked his men along slowly, staying well hidden. They stopped at one spot to scrutinize the ranch-house and listen to the thirsty horses.

"The three dead men are still there," said Stark.

"You can mighty near hear the flies buzzin'," said one of the Nottings.

They worked a little farther until they came to the edge of the timber. Blake spoke in a low voice. "Mark the corrals and the buildings. It's almost dark. In another half hour it will be pitch black. You Nottings, I want you to sneak down there as soon as it gets dark and quietly open the corrals so the horses can get out and go to water. I don't want any horses left for anybody to ride away from that house. *Sabe?*"

The brothers nodded.

"If anybody comes after a horse —" Blake shook his head.

Stark said, "The Indian girl's horse went down to the creek already."

Blake began to whittle at the base of a young pine about two inches in diameter.

"When the break comes, you'll see about fifty hombres runnin' hell-bent for election toward the creek, and I imagine they'll be making some fireworks with their hardware."

"And then we close in behind and shoot them from the rear," Stark said eagerly.

Blake shook his head. He squatted on his heels, chewing a stem of bunch grass, straining his eyes through the quickly gathering twilight to watch the house. "We won't be able to see them. It'll be dark — remember?"

Stark looked disappointed.

"There is at least one wounded man in the house, and watch out for him. He'll be dangerous."

"We're going in the house?" asked Stark.

"That's right." He looked around at them all. "They may not all head for the creek," he said. "If any stay behind, we want to be there."

"Wait a minute," said one of the Nottings. "You figure Tinley won't be in the breakout for the creek. He'll stay behind, and maybe he'll count on getting a horse so he can get out of the valley."

"It's a good guess," said Blake.

"That don't jibe with what you said in Mountain City. You said if anybody went after Tinley, somebody would get killed."

"That's still true — *if* you tree him. But don't ever doubt that Tinley will look out for his own hide first."

"I always figured he was the kind that wouldn't like to run."

"He doesn't — if he's got first draw. But when it comes right down to it, Tinley is for anything that will protect his skin, or buy him the things he wants." Blake got up. His left leg was stiff. He had washed it off in the creek and tied his bandanna around it, and it hadn't bothered him much all day, but now it was beginning to ache. He'd have to keep walking, he guessed, or it would stiffen up. He nodded at the Notting brothers. "Better get down there — but don't take any chances. Don't be seen unless you run smack into somebody."

"What about Red Flynn and his men?"

"We'll leave them there for a while in case Tinley's men manage to hold the ranch-house."

"What's going to happen if the sheriff deals himself a hand in this?" asked Stark.

Blake stared at him. "That was a good question to ask yourselves last night."

CHAPTER NINETEEN

"We-ell —" Stark didn't finish; for the first time he was giving some real thought to the affair in which he was involved.

The Nottings too looked at Stark. Blake watched them.

"We're in a fix," Stark said slowly.

Blake said, "You were in a fix when the first homesteader moved to Crazyman. Anybody who knew Tinley could have told you that. Tinley is no compromiser. He wants things his way."

One of the other men spoke up. "Look here, Summers. They say Tinley chased you out of Albany County some years ago, about the time Tom Horn was hanged. That right?"

"I left Albany County because I did not want to do any more killing."

"It sounds good the way you say it," said Stark, "but somehow it all adds up to the same thing: you and Tinley were feudin', and you got out of the country."

"You can look at it any way you like, I figure."

"But where does that put us now? Are you tryin' to organize us so you can get back at Tinley?"

Blake said impatiently, "I didn't organize you. You were ganged up there by the watering trough howling for Tinley's scalp when I rode up. I stopped you from going after him because I knew somebody would be killed — and knowing Tinley, I figured it wouldn't be him."

"So you went after Tinley yourself."

A pause. "But you didn't get him," said one of the Nottings.

"No," said Stark flatly. "He got away."

"And now we're all here, doing what you say," said the third man.

Blake looked at them. So now they were thinking, and now they were scared. They had embarked on this deadly business without considering the consequences, but now, in the final throes of the fight, they were weighing the various factors judiciously.

Blake said, "Why did you come up the valley in the first place?"

"Because he burned cabins and run off stock."

"Has that changed?"

Stark didn't answer.

"Nothing is changed," Blake went on, "but the way you feel. You aren't as rambunctious now as you were last night."

"I still can't understand why you let Tinley get away. This whole business could have been wrapped up if you had stopped him last night."

"Maybe I wasn't quick enough on the draw."

"You was quick enough when you shot John Wall," Notting pointed out.

Blake considered. There was no point in arguing with men who were scared of what they had done and what they were about to do. The main thing was, they would have felt all right about tearing up the valley in a big frontal assault that would have killed or wounded half of them before they had time to think it over, but now, in the cold light of fourteen hours of inaction, they were ready to call it quits and go home to their warm beds.

"Anybody here without a family?" asked Blake.

Nobody answered.

"I might have figured," Blake said aciduously, "that you would turn chicken when you got to the real thing."

Notting said slowly, "It seems different now, somehow. Before, we were part of a big bunch. Now there's only a few of us, and we're going to the ranch-house. If there's somebody there, we'll have to kill them, according to you. Isn't that it?"

"You've sure got to be ready to kill — if you don't want to *be* killed." Blake had the sapling almost whittled in two. He broke it off cautiously so it wouldn't crack. Then he went up about two feet from the end and began to whittle through again.

"What happens if I run onto Tinley myself," asked Stark, "and I kill him? I'm the one to face the grand jury then."

Blake said caustically, "You figured that as long as you were one of a mob, and nobody could know who fired the exact shot that did the killing, you could get out with a whole hide. But now that it's straight up to you, you're scared."

Nobody answered. Blake cut through the sapling and began to trim off the small branches. A moment later he closed his knife and put it in his pants pocket. He swung the club and it felt right. It was green and had weight; it was tough and wouldn't break. He stood up and dusted the seat of his pants. "It was something to think about last night — and that was a hell of a lot better time to back out than now. It's dark," he announced. "I'm going down to the corrals." He stepped toward the ranch-house. His left leg almost buckled, but he kept it under him. He bent down and pretended to pick up a stone and toss it away on the soft bed of pine needles.

"I'm going," said the fourth man.

Blake looked around, still keeping his voice low. "Anybody who feels doubtful about this, stay back here. We may need coverage from this side anyhow. If anybody is really ready to go with me, let's get moving."

The fourth man came forward, a six-shooter in his right hand, a knife in his belt. Blake looked him over in the rapidly darkening twilight. He was a man about Blake's own age, clean shaven, with a long face and a projecting jaw. "What's your name?" asked Blake.

"Wyeth — lower end of Gunsmoke."

"All right, Wyeth, let's get going before the breakout comes and finds us sitting on our tails."

Stark got up, holding his rifle. "I'll open the corrals," he said, "like I promised."

Blake glanced at him. If the man had had a coonskin cap, he could have been a Kentucky frontiersman a hundred years before. Blake said, "All right. The rest of you stay here and cover us."

"Both of them corrals open on the south," said Stark. "I'll go around the south side."

"Watch your step. Somebody from the ranch-house may have some ideas about those horses."

"I'll watch," said Stark.

"No shooting until you have to."

Stark slid away in the darkness. It was still twilight up on the mountain tops, but down here in the valley it was black night. Blake led the way around the left side of the corrals. He went slowly, to give the Washakie hands time.

He stopped while he was still covered by the corral, and put his hand back to hold Wyeth. It was now so dark in the bottom of the valley that he could make out the ranch-house only by its silhouette against the stars. He saw momentary flickers of light, and knew he had it figured right. The men were checking their equipment, getting ready for a move.

He heard no sound from the other side of the corral, but the horses began to trot around in a circle, and in a moment he knew that Stark was chousing them into the open. He heard a neigh, and, crouched low, saw the loping forms against the dark background of the meadow.

Still there was no sound from Stark. The man was, in truth, a woodsman. A horned toad was noisy by the side of him. Presently there was that sense of swift, circular movement from the second corral, and Blake moved up. The stock was draining out of it. With his ear close to the ground, Blake heard the drumming of hooves across the hard-packed earth.

Then Blake came upon the first thing he had not really anticipated. A horse just outside of the corral, hearing the others go to water, neighed vehemently. Blake froze. That horse had not been outside half an hour before.

He watched, trying to adjust his eyes to the darkness, to make out any dark shape that had no business being there. Presently, by the horse's head, he saw a tall hat. He crept a step closer. He saw the outline of the man's face, pointed toward the corral gate, and he knew the man was wondering what in hell had turned loose all the horses.

Now Blake was in a spot. This fellow was on the other side of the horse, and it wasn't going to be easy to get to him. He didn't dare duck under the horse's neck, for he would be vulnerable, and he didn't want to go around the horse, for he would have to make a big circle to keep away from the horse's heels.

He got to the horse's side and rose slowly to look over the saddle. He started to bring up his club, but the horse swung its head and whickered, and the club struck it under the jaw. The horse reared, and a deafening burst of yellow flame came from under the horse's neck.

The horse reared again, and Stark's tall, dark form came in silently from behind the man. There was the sound of a knife cutting through meat and tissue. Wind whistled out of the man's voice box once before he went down.

A voice called from the house: "You all right, Shep?"

Blake answered, his voice muffled against his sleeve: "All right." He was thankful that Red was holding his fire up above, though he had figured if shooting broke out, Red would know enough to lay off. He whispered behind him, "Wyeth?"

Wyeth whispered back, "That'n scorched my shoulder, but I'm all right."

The horse was trying to get loose to head for water, but Blake left it tied. It might make good bait. He moved under the horse's neck and stepped across the dead man. "I stuck my neck out now," Stark whispered. "I might as well go along."

Wyeth whispered behind him, "You reckon them four will cover us?"

Blake asked, "How can they, in the dark?"

He stayed low, with one hand on the horse's knee to detect movement that would indicate somebody else coming from the ranch-house.

Then the breakout came. From the doors and windows at the front of the ranch-house poured a mass of yelling, shooting men. In a moment they were within Blake's vision, heading for the creek. Powder-flash after powder-flash showed the meadow apparently filled with running men, all headed for the creek. The narrow valley was filled with the thunderous roll of six-shooters and the sharp crack of carbines. There were a few answering flashes from the creek. Then the heavy smoke settled down like a fog, and Blake could see nothing but occasional flashes within it. The body of men was moving toward the creek, and Blake wondered how many, if any, had stayed behind with Tinley.

He found out. The back of the ranch-house suddenly spewed out men. They ran hard but without sound. There were no shots. And they came for the corrals.

Blake's lips tightened. So this was Tinley's tactic — and it was a good one. The main body of men made a feint for the creek, but they knew as well as anybody that they needed horses, so now fifteen or twenty men were coming on a dead run for the corrals.

There was no time for thinking. If Blake had had his six men with him, he would have been in position to put up a fight, but now he had two — one on each side of him, spread out across the yard. He fired two shots at a running form and jumped an instant after. For one brief moment there was no answer. Then hell broke loose as six-shooters bucked all over the yard at the same time, and hot lead poured into the hole where Blake had been.

"Back!" Blake shouted, and ducked for the cover of the corrals. He sensed motion beside him, and knew that Stark and Wyeth were with him.

When the yard was lighted up with the explosions, Blake looked back and saw how the Washakie men were spread out. They had been looking for an ambush, or they would have made a beeline for the corral gates.

The one horse tied to the corral was rearing and snorting, nervous from thirst and frightened by the fireworks. Blake ducked behind it. Wyeth and Stark were just ahead of him. Bullets were hunting them out as the advancing gunfighters tried to shoot them down before the powder smoke closed in. Blake saw Stark stumble and skid forward on his face, the back of his head blown off by a heavy bullet. Wyeth was streaking on around the corral. Blake felt blood running down his neck, but he didn't move.

The shooting stopped as abruptly as it had broken out. Blake waited. A dark form came around the horse's hind quarters on tiptoe. Blake raised the club slowly, silently, and brought it down hard. The man dropped like a stuck hog.

Another one came under the horse's neck, and Blake spun, caving in the man's forehead with the club as the pistol exploded and the bullet jerked at Blake's shirt under his left arm. He heard a struggle going on across the corral, and made his way back there as cautiously as he could. The hands seemed to be converging on the corral gate.

Wyeth was fighting two or three men. Blake circled them but he couldn't tell who was who. Then one of them shot at Wyeth, and Blake saw the picture. Wyeth's face was covered with blood. He was hacking with his knife and backing away.

Blake's club cracked against the skull of the man who had fired. He jammed his .44 into the side of the man next to him, pulled it back a few inches, and let it go. The man dropped; his woolen shirt began burning in a small area.

The third man turned to Blake, and Wyeth got him from behind. For one instant they were alone. Blake said, “Come on!” and led the way back to the saddled horse.

But the horse was left to itself. The men from the ranch-house, having scoured the corrals and found nothing, began moving back toward the ranch-house. Somebody shouted, “Make for the creek!” and in an instant they were like a herd of steers with their tails curled, stampeding across the meadow.

Blake took a deep breath. This was what he had been awaiting. Tinley would never be in that bunch. As sure as the Lord made little apples, Tinley was waiting for the shooting to die down. That saddled horse was for him.

Blake took his knife and cut the reins. The horse jerked his head, found he was free, and trotted off around the house. Blake moved toward the back door and waited on one side. Wyeth waited on the other.

The door opened slowly. A man came out. Blake hit him on the back of the head. The man went down. Blake struck a match, held it for an instant, then threw it away as a pistol shot blazed from the window. The man on the ground was not Tinley, but now Wyeth grunted, holding his hand to his stomach, and went down slowly.

The door was still open. Blake stepped out of his boots and across the threshold. A board creaked under him. A shot came from across the room, and Blake fired above the blaze. At his second shot he saw the other man. He looked as if somebody had thrown a bottle of catsup in his face. Blake's pistol dropped slowly. He moved to one side in the dark. Again a board creaked, but nothing else happened. Without further movement he scanned the rooms, getting the powder flash out of his eyes and the deafening crash of the explosion out of his ears. Tinley was somewhere in this house; he felt sure of that.

Outside, there was whooping at the creek, and Blake thought the Washakie hands were catching up as many horses as possible. He hoped his guards, upstream and downstream, would be cautious.

He heard padded steps in the cellar below, and knew that somebody was walking on a dirt floor. Then there was silence.

Outside, sporadic, far-away rifle shots came from across the valley, and he knew that Art Powell was keeping the Washakie hands occupied. A stray bullet whined over the ranch-house in a ricochet, and he heard occasional shots from Red Flynn, high up on the rocks. Apparently Red had sized up the situation correctly, and was putting pressure on the Washakie men from behind. It could get warm out there, Blake thought. The Washakie hands might even decide to retreat to the ranch-house.

He heard galloping horses, and two shots sounded as the horses went down the valley. A moment later came more shots. The downstream guards had closed in. Blake listened. The galloping horses came back up the road. One of them went back to the creek. The other veered off and slowed down. The night in the valley was very quiet for a moment.

Then a hootowl sounded off, high up on Poison Mountain. The sound came down to the ranch-house, so clear that it was startling for an instant. A coyote howled on the rim above Blake's place. Firing broke out again along the creek and from the hills on the other side — red and yellow eruptions in the night, thunderous explosions or the whine of rifle bullets.

Still Blake waited. There was somebody in the cellar; he knew that. And they would have to come out eventually. Then he heard something scraping over the board floor.

He wheeled and moved soundlessly to one side. He made the move successfully but he crashed into the kitchen stove. It knocked him off balance. A shot crashed almost in his face. He felt the burns from the powder, but he kept falling away. In that brief glimpse from the light of the explosion he had seen Cotton Stewart, white-haired, red-faced, his bare chest covered with blood from the wound he had got in the yard. He was on his hands and knees, terrible pain distorting his face as he tried again to raise his pistol for a shot.

Blake rolled on the floor and regained his feet. He stood for an instant and spotted Stewart's harsh breathing. He swung his leg, and his foot came up under Stewart's wrist. The man's pistol thudded on the ceiling, clattered down, and came to rest in a corner. Stewart cursed him painfully and died.

Blake was near the cellarway now. The door, which was made to lie flat with the floor, had been opened back until it rested on the seat of a chair, and the faint light still came from below, but from where he was, Blake could see nothing but a dirt wall.

Blake thought he was in a fairly safe position. He now covered the door through which Cotton Stewart had crawled, and he also covered the door to the back. If anybody came up the cellarway he would make a perfect target. There was only — Blake stiffened.

He heard the pounding of horses' hooves coming up from the creek. There were at least two horses. Blake frowned in the dark. What now? Then he heard more hooves, many more, and he knew that his trap had been too good. The Washakie hands, their stomachs full of cold water and their bellies full of hot lead, were retreating to the ranch-house. They had been fired upon from the road and they didn't know how many men had been there; for all they knew, there might have been forty or fifty. Apparently they assumed too that Blake had a guard on the upper portion, or perhaps they had sent men up there and drawn fire. At any rate, a full scale retreat was now in progress, and within three or four minutes the ranch-house would be either filled with Washakie hands or surrounded by them.

If Tinley was in that cellar, Blake would have to move fast, for Tinley had to be dead before they got back. Tinley's death was the only thing that would settle this fight.

For one instant Blake turned to the back door. There was time to get away. But the man responsible for the burning and killing was in the cellar. Blake tiptoed across the floor.

He got on his knees, then on his stomach. With his pistol in his right hand and his club in the left, he crawled forward, digging his elbows into the floor, pushing with his toes.

He held the pistol even with his eyes, for he didn't want to give a shot until he could return one. A two-by-six ran alongside the opening cut for the door, to support the floor. Blake was down two steps before he could see under it.

Then he saw Tinley: he saw that hunted look on the man's face, the white spots just below his temples. He saw shelves full of canned goods; a table in the center with a kerosene lamp on it; two chairs. In that brief instant he saw also an open bottle of whisky on the table. Then he aimed at Tinley and pulled the trigger. His first shot went over Tinley's shoulder into a can of tomatoes. Then there was only a metallic click. The pistol was empty.

Tinley had his pistol up now, and he grinned sardonically. Then a buckskin-clad figure came out of a corner. Soft Hands threw herself at Tinley's shooting arm.

Tinley swore and beat at her face with the butt of the pistol.

Blake didn't hesitate. He put his hands on the step below his face, turned a full somersault through the air, and landed on his stocking feet at the bottom of the stair. He threw his club in to his right hand and sprang at Tinley.

Soft Hands was in a pile on the floor, her face hidden in her arms, blood pouring over the buckskin. Tinley fired at Blake, but he fired too fast. The shot went wild, and Blake closed with him.

The man was desperate. Blake couldn't hold him. Tinley brought up the pistol again, and Blake struck his hand with the club. Tinley showed no pain. He refused to let go. Blake dropped the club and leaped for Tinley's arm.

The shot plowed up dirt at Blake's feet. Blake forced the man against the canned goods, but Tinley got one foot behind him and came back savagely. A bullet creased Blake's shoulder. He backed into the table and the lamp went over, spilling kerosene on the floor. This caught fire, and the yellow flames licked up, with long streamers of soot at their tops.

Their fighting space was about four by ten feet. Once again Blake rushed at Tinley. This time he took a bullet along the ribs, but he got his hands on the pistol and tore it away from Tinley. He had intended to use it, but his jerk was so violent that the pistol got away from him and landed in the middle of the pool of burning kerosene.

Tinley came at him, teeth bared for biting. Blake hammered the teeth back in his face. He cut his knuckles but he didn't mind.

The pistol roared at his side, and a can of peaches exploded over Tinley's head. The heat of the fire had detonated the cartridge. The pistol spun and bucked and roared again. Blake didn't see where the shot went. He staggered Tinley. The man fell backward into the shelves, and the entire rack of canned goods fell over on him. Blake started to pull the man out of the pile. Then he looked around. The stairway was on fire.

He glanced at the Indian girl. She would be a load, he thought. He picked her up in his arms. She was limp, as if unconscious. Her head, flung back on his arm, was mutilated from the gunwhipping and covered with blood. Blake vaulted up the stairway. He laid her on the floor and started back down.

But he was met with a billowing gust of yellow fire. He threw up his arms to save his face. The flames poured out of the cellar, and he knew they would not stop. Blake picked up the Shoshone girl again and carried her through the door. Men were dismounting.

"Tinley's in the cellar!" Blake shouted.

They started in, but they came back out. Blake carried the girl as far as the corral and laid her down. She still didn't move.

A corner of the kitchen burst into flames. Cans of food began exploding. The outside began to be lighted up, and suddenly shots began to pour down from above into the men who had retreated. Shots came from across the creek. Still more Washakie men ran up to the burning house on foot, but were met by fire from Red Flynn and from the four men Blake had left behind.

Blake himself crouched in the shelter of the corral. He saw blood on his right arm, but he didn't seem to be hit. Two men went down in the Washakie group. They tried to go back to the creek, but were met with gunfire from Art Powell's men.

The Washakie ranch-house was ablaze from top to bottom, and lighted up the whole valley. Tinley's gunfighters were trapped. One raised his hands high, and others followed. In a few seconds, at least forty men were back to back in a tight little group, their hands raised, milling like a bunch of cattle in the light from the burning ranch-house.

The shooting stopped. Blake waited until the men came up from the creek. When Art Powell's men reached the surrendering party, Blake got up slowly and went forward. He said, "Take their guns and knives and boots and turn 'em loose."

"Where's Tinley?" asked Chet White.

Blake pointed. "In there — in the cellar."

Chet White looked and shook his head. Blake said to Art, "Did you lose any?"

"One," said Art. "Luke Leslie got it between the eyes on a shot in the dark. Two men got hit but not serious."

One of the Nottings came into the light. "How about Stark and Wyeth?"

Blake looked stonily at him. "They came with me," he said pointedly, "and died."

Red came up. "You look like you been in a sausage grinder," he said.

"I came through," said Blake, suddenly beginning to feel tired.

"Where'd you leave your boots?" asked Horton.

Blake pointed. "Just outside the door. I don't sup —" He wheeled. "Somebody take care of the Indian girl," he said. "She got beat up pretty bad."

Red Flynn went over to her. He straightened her out a little, then came back to Blake. "She's dead," he said. "Shot through the neck."

"Shot?" Blake remembered then the six-shooter in the burning kerosene, bucking and firing. He shook his head.

"You need a doctor," said Art Powell.

"I need a smoke," said Blake, and began to fish for makin's just as he keeled over.

CHAPTER TWENTY

They bandaged the wounded; Blake had bandannas all over him. They found shovels and set the prisoners to digging graves. They buried the eight Washakie men, and Luke Leslie, Stark, and Wyeth. Cotton Stewart and J. J. Tinley could be assumed dead after the roof fell in on the huge Washakie headquarters house.

The homesteaders herded the disarmed survivors of the Star Under a Roof brand down the valley, past scattered herds of cattle and gray spots with blackened stumps standing up to mark the sites of cabins and sheds.

They were sober groups that morning as the sun lighted up the yellow rocks on the northwest side of the valley. They rode at a walk, the Washakie men surrounded by homesteaders armed with rifles and revolvers.

"We've got no use for you," Blake told them. "There's no way we can collect our damages from you. Not a one of you has got more than enough money to get out of town. Most of you don't own the horses you are riding or the saddles on them. We're keeping your arms and seeing you into town. After that, you better scatter. Tinley is dead. Cotton Stewart is dead. There's nobody to pay you, nobody to back you up."

"What about our back pay?" asked one slant-jawed gunfighter.

"How much have you got coming?"

"Three months — a hundred and eighty dollars."

"My advice to you is to get out of town. You can send in your claim to the probate court by mail."

The slant-jawed man bristled. "Why get out of town? I've got as much right in Mountain City as you have."

"You sure have. Maybe more," Blake conceded. "But how are you going to explain drawing sixty dollars a month as a hand? That's fighting pay — and some people might remember *that* when they start rebuilding their homes."

Red Flynn dropped off to look after the Pronghorn cattle. Chet White stayed back to look after his stock. One of the Crawfords dropped out, and old man Horton delegated one of his hands to stay behind. There was only big stock left — horses, cattle, and a few hogs on Luke Leslie's place. Another of the Crawfords decided to look after Luke's outfit. Down at Horton's, the chicken house had been fired along with everything else, and the stench of half-burned chickens made the valley stink like a slaughter house.

Art Powell rode up beside Blake. "What are we going to do when we get into town?"

"It isn't our move," Blake said. He jogged along for a moment. "I'll see Doc Adams and make a report on all the dead ones. The rest is up to the authorities."

They crossed the sagebrush flat — close to a hundred weary, powder-grimed horsemen. The sun was up but it wasn't warm this morning.

"Be an early fall," Powell said.

"Probably." Blake was busy with his thoughts. He watched the Washakie gunfighters sifting through the sagebrush, and he traveled in their dust. He was still riding in his sock feet, and the cool air coming down across the sagebrush from the northwest felt good to his aching muscles. A flight of sagehens thundered up on the right and flew heavily into the sun, but nobody even took a shot at them.

Blake turned once and looked back up the valley. The morning mist had lifted, and there was little to show from this distance the havoc that had been created the night before except for a few slowly rising spirals of thin smoke. Blake turned back.

They rode down the main street of Mountain City. Shopkeepers stared at them. The harness-maker with his leather apron looked at the army of mounted men and rubbed his eyes and looked again. The postmaster, up early to catch the stage from the west, came to the door and watched them ride by. Every door and every window held a face, but there were no greetings.

The Washakie hands kept straight up the main street. Blake was riding at the head of the homesteaders, head up, jaw hard. There was still much to come. There had been killing; there would be settling. He stopped the homesteaders a block from the watering trough and let the Washakie men water their horses. Then they began to disperse, and in a moment the street was empty. Blake led his men forward to the trough.

At that moment a small girl — maybe eight years old — came skipping out from between the bakery and the general store with a gallon bucket in her hand. She started across the street, looked up and saw the advancing horsemen, and stood stone still for an instant. Then her mouth dropped open. She turned to run back, then changed her mind. She started across the street but tripped and fell flat on her face in the dust. The bucket flew out in front of her and sprayed milk over the street.

Old man Horton picked her up. She was crying by that time. He rinsed out her bucket in the watering trough, gave her a quarter, and sent her back to the bakery for more milk.

The tension broke. The men watered their horses and began to spread out through the sagebrush, heading for home. Blake sent Docie and the other wounded men up to Adams' office over the bank. He took his roan to the livery stable. At least twenty horses with the Star Under a Roof brand were in the back, munching hay — most of them still saddled, bridles hanging from the saddlehorns.

"Lot of business this morning," Blake said.

"Most I ever saw in Mountain City." Carthy looked at him with his one eye, but Blake didn't feel like talking. He got down, still wearing his six-shooter, and gave the reins to Carthy. The one-eyed man said, "Long night."

"Pretty long," said Blake, and set off down the street toward the harness shop.

"You got a pair of boots I can wear?" he asked the old man with the leather apron.

The old man looked at his feet and sized them up. "I think so — if you take off that bandage."

Blake sat down on a pile of sole leather. The old man brought a boot. "What happened to your'n?" he asked.

"They got burned," said Blake.

The boots fitted. Blake had enough money to pay him, with some left over. He walked across the street to the saloon. Art Powell was having a couple, and a bunch of ex-Washakie hands were drinking silently in a huddle at a table in the back.

The bartender set out a bottle. "What happened up on Crazyman last night?" he asked. "Everybody come in peaceful-like this morning, but them fellers" — he cast a glance at the ex-Washakie hands — "ain't got no hardware."

Blake tossed his drink down. "Maybe they aren't in the hardware business," he said.

The bartender looked disappointed.

"By the way," said Blake, "you keep a gun-belt back there for Tinley, don't you?"

"Well, yes — I — he told me to. That is — it's his saloon, you know."

Blake looked at him for a moment. "You better wrap up that gun-belt and put it away," he said. "For keeps."

The bartender's mouth dropped open. Blake had another drink. Then he said to Art Powell, "Hope you aren't aiming to start a ruckus with that bunch back there?"

Powell had another one. "I'm just trying to get up courage to face the old lady," he said.

Blake went out. "So long," he said to Art.

He went up the street to Conway's office. Conway was brushing the dust from his front window. "I'll see you in a minute," he said.

"Take your time." Blake went in and sat down and started to look for makin's, but he decided he was too tired. He sat there, legs sprawled out, arms draped over the chair arms, and went to sleep almost immediately.

"— some trouble up on Crazyman," Conway was saying.

Blake opened his eyes. For a moment he didn't move. Then he sat up straight. "Some," he said. "But I came here to give myself up for the killing of John Wall."

Conway put the dust rag away in a bottom drawer of his desk. "I heard something about that. Were there any witnesses?"

"Homer Mohr of Cheyenne and one of the Crawford brothers. I can't say which one."

"Well, I suppose as U.S. commissioner I am empowered to accept your surrender. Want to give me your gun?"

Blake unbuckled the belt, rolled it up with the gun inside, and handed it over.

"Maybe," said Conway, "you better let me look into this for a couple of hours, just to be sure there's something to hold you for." He looked at the rolled gun-belt. “You came in and surrendered, so I don’t reckon you’ll try to run away. Why don’t you come back about dinner time?”

Blake started to get up.

“By the way,” said Conway, “last night in the mail I got a letter from Washington. The U.S. Supreme Court has decided that contracts made with Indians are valid and must be honored.” He looked at Blake from under his eyebrows. “You know what that means?”

“No.”

“The government made a treaty with the Shoshones in 1868, guaranteeing them use of the Wind River Reservation, including the right to the water originating thereon for irrigation or other purposes. That right, as I think I told you last spring, had not been fully exercised, and a few years ago a suit was started to declare the right null and void for non-use. Most of us expected the Supreme Court would uphold this view — but they have not. The way it stacks up now, the Shoshones are probably entitled to all the water originating on the reservation.”

“But Crazyman has been opened to settlement. It isn’t in the reservation any more.”

“True enough — but you forget one thing. This land that the United States got from the Indians a few years ago belongs to the United States until it is filed on.”

Blake frowned. “In other words, the state has no jurisdiction over it or over the water on it.”

“That’s right.”

“Then the re-classification of water originating on upper Crazyman has no legal standing at all.”

"That's the way it looks under this new decision."
"And the water belongs to the Indians?"
"Hard to say. They sold the land, and presumably the water rights went with it. However, a number of Indian families have filed on homesteads on the upper portion of Crazyman Creek, above the valley itself. It is up in there that the creek originates from the melting of snow. It is going to be a neat question as to who owns what water rights, but I would say offhand that Indian rights are going to come ahead of municipal use or any other use derived from state law." He looked at Blake carefully. "So," he said, "what's the use of all the fighting?"
"The fighting is done," Blake said presently, "and over nothing, as fighting is sometimes."
"Always," Conway said firmly.
Blake corrected him. "Not always. There are many times when fighting clears the air, when it settles feuds by killing off the feuders. In a new country, those who take rights generally keep them. I have seen it happen many times, and it is not often that the courts reverse possession of a right as it has done here with the Indians."
"It was wasted this time."
"Maybe." Blake got up. "Maybe ridding the state of Wyoming of a man was worth a whole lot. He made a lot of lives miserable while he lived."
"Will they be any better off now?"
"Not right away — but eventually."
He dropped into the saloon again. Art Powell was gone. The Washakie men were gone.

Blake backed out.

"Hold on a minute," said the bartender. "It's time for the house to buy a drink."

"It's been time for a long time," Blake observed.

"Men coming in here all morning. Powder stains on their faces and hands, blood-soaked bandages — what went on up there on Crazyman?"

Blake killed the drink. "You got a new boss," he said.

This did not grieve the bartender. "Who is it?"

"Don't know. Maybe his widow, maybe most anybody. Maybe he didn't leave anything in the clear. Hard to tell about a man who lives the way he did."

Blake walked down the street toward the harness shop again. He saw Roberta Blendick's head bent over her drawing board, and went inside.

"Morning, ma'am," he said.

She looked up and gasped. "You've been hit!"

"No, ma'am. Just scratched a time or two. Thought I ought to drop in before I pull out," he said.

"You're going away?"

"What else? They burned everything I owned, including my wagon and harness. All I've got left is my stock. The water rights are gone, so far as I can see, and anyway I don't think I'll like it in Crazyman any more. There'll always be a smell there from the skunk who burned us out."

"Somebody will live on that land."

"I doubt it, ma'am — not until the water rights question gets settled. If the government takes a notion to impound the spring overflow waters, which it well might, our land is worthless. We're better off to hunt up some new land while it's still available. I imagine the Land Office will cancel our filings and let us go somewhere else."

Roberta laid down her pen carefully, then turned to him. "Blake —" She was getting up.

The door opened and a tiny woman in a brown silk dress came in, followed by four children. "I'm sorry," she said to Roberta, "but you're the only person I know to talk to in Mountain City. Where do you suggest I can rent a light wagon to drive up to the Washakie place? I haven't much money," she added, "but my husband's credit should be good."

Blake stared at her. He never had seen her before last night. He looked at the oldest girl — about fourteen, wearing a checked gingham dress, a straw hat with a long ribbon, dark red hair in braids, and long black stockings. He looked at the other two girls, at the small boy Mrs. Tinley was holding by the hand.

Blake took off his hat. "Ma'am," he said, "I take it you're looking for J. J. Tinley."

"Yes," she said eagerly. "Do you know him?"

Blake took a deep breath. "Some," he said. He doubted that anybody knew all about Tinley.

"How is he? Have you seen him lately?"

Blake's eyes half closed. He hated what he had to do. "I can give you news of Tinley," he said, "but it isn't very good news."

Her face dropped. "What has he done? Has he — was it another woman?" she asked suddenly.

It wasn't hard to lie. "Your husband had an accident," he said.

The woman's face went white. She came close to Blake. Her voice was small but steady. "What kind of accident, please?"

"He got caught under some falling timbers," Blake said. "He — it — he never knew."

Tears rolled down the small woman's cheeks. She compressed her lips almost painfully. "Thank God! He didn't suffer!"

Blake stood silent. Roberta put her arm around the woman, and her other around the oldest girl. "Sit down here, please," said Roberta. "You'll be all right."

She looked over the woman's shoulder at Blake, and nodded toward her desk. Blake got the smelling salts.

Suddenly the woman went all to pieces and began to sob with great, rending cries. Blake got the children outside. The harness-maker's wife came hurrying out of the little shop, and Blake told her what was the trouble.

"I'll take care of the children," she said at once.

Blake stood there for a moment. Mrs. Tinley didn't have much money. Obviously she had spent all she had to come up on the train to visit her husband. Blake didn't know where Tinley had kept her hidden, but probably back in Albany County. Nevertheless, she had dressed herself and her children in their best and had come to see him.

Blake walked back up the street to the bank. Perry Miller was sweeping out his little office. He looked up and said, "Howdy, Blake. Come in and find a chair."

Blake said, "You know that Tinley is dead?"

The banker pushed a few papers on his desk. "I heard that."

"His widow is here in town, and she hasn't got enough money to get back home. What can you do for her?"

Perry Miller's gray tufts of whiskers bobbed up. "His widow?"

"His widow — and four children."

Miller scrutinized Blake. "There's no question about Tinley's being dead?"

"None. He was almost unconscious and he was caught under a hundred gallon cans of tomatoes in the cellar. The ranch-house was on fire and there wasn't time to get him out. I watched it burn. Nobody came out of that house."

Miller leaned back. "The bank has a mortgage on everything that carries the Washakie brand," he said finally. "All stock, all buildings and equipment, all feed stored there. We also hold a mortgage on the saloon and the hotel. I doubt there will be a penny left over when our mortgages are satisfied."

Blake was astounded. "Surely he didn't live up to every cent he made."

Miller shrugged. "Unless he put it in the sock. How can you keep twenty or thirty men on at fighting wages and make any money?"

"That wouldn't be the whole story."

"Probably not. I have observed that when a man spends extravagantly in one place, he is likely to in other places. That is why the bank was so careful to keep itself protected — and with good reason, I think."

"Well," said Blake, "I haven't taken out my feed yet, and I still have my cattle. Maybe you better let me have fifty dollars on that loan."

"What for?" Miller asked bluntly.

"There's a woman here," Blake said, "a nice little woman. Her hands are rough from farm work, but there's still a light in her eyes when she mentions J. J. Tinley. She's his wife, and her four kids are his kids. She came up here to visit him, and now she hasn't got enough money to get back home."

Miller's eyebrows lifted. "It won't be necessary for you to handle that personally, Blake. You've forgotten something. You handed me Tinley's Waldorf bag with $23,000 in it. Nobody has come forward to claim that — and far as the bank is concerned, we'll try to get our money out of the Washakie Land & Cattle Company. Anyway, we have no way of knowing to whom this money belonged — whether it was Tinley's personally, or the company's. You said you took it from John Wall, but far as I know, it might belong to you." He reached down into the kneehole of his desk and lifted the bag. "I'd be willing to turn it over to you for a purpose like that. Seems to me the widow ought to have *something*."

Blake got up. It was the first lift he had felt in thirty-six hours. "I'll take it to her," he said. "With your compliments."

"Not mine. I'm not in the business of charity."

"Any way you want to put it." He started out. But Conway was coming in, followed by half a dozen others. "Stay around, Summers," he said. "This concerns you."

Summers sat down again.

"We come up here to hold a meeting," Conway said to Miller, "and see what you think."

"There are more chairs outside," said Miller.

They got seated. One man stood against the door. Conway faced Miller across the table. "There's been a homesteader's war," he said. "It was provoked by the Washakie crew. The homesteaders fought back, and it looks like they come out on top. There were men killed on both sides. This is going to call for a grand jury action."

"Conceivably," Miller murmured.

"But we got other things to think about," said Conway.

"Name them," said Miller.

"This fight was provoked by Tinley. Everybody knows that. These men did only what anyone would have done under the circumstances. It's happened a lot of times in the West."

"That's no excuse for condoning murder," said Miller.

"We're not suggesting it be condoned. Look at it this way. Forty or fifty men are involved — mostly heads of families. We can't throw these men in jail until a trial. I suggest we tell them all to stay on their places and keep at work. Their families have got to be fed; their stock has got to be taken care of." He paused. "The bank has plenty of mortgages on property belonging to these men, hasn't it?"

"The bank has wide-spread interests," Miller admitted.

"We're not here to say killing is right or wrong, or even that this particular killing is justified. But I've lived here for twenty years, Perry. I was selling fire insurance before the bank was organized. I know these men, upright, God-fearing men who work hard and take care of their families."

"And?"

"There'll have to be a grand jury. But we can get together and send a petition to Governor Brooks asking him to grant a blanket amnesty for everybody involved."

Miller looked up. "Think he'll do it?"

"I was raised on the same ranch with Bryant Brooks; I saved his hair from the Sioux. If I ask him, he'll do it. But I won't ask him unless the leading businessmen of Mountain City are agreed. It is my opinion that these men should be allowed to go back to their homesteads without fear of prosecution. It's time for the people in this area to get back to work and cut out this fighting — and I for one am in favor of giving them assurance."

Blake sat there with his hat pushed back and watched them all. There were a lot of personal motivations involved, sure. You move forty or fifty families out of the country and Mountain City would shrivel and die. But there was justice in it, too, for one rotten apple in the barrel — J. J. Tinley — had been at the bottom of the trouble.

Perry Miller was thinking it over. Finally he looked up at Conway. "I'll go along," he said.

"Thanks." Conway went out, followed by his men. Blake got up with the bag. At the front door Conway turned back. "I looked into the death of John Wall," he said. "Crawford claims Wall drew first."

"What about Mohr?"

Conway grunted. "Mohr left on the stage last night for Thermopolis. My guess is you'll never hear another word out of him. Mohr's in too deep; he doesn't dare start anything."

Blake drew a deep breath. "That sure sounds good," he said.

He went up the street to Roberta's office. Mrs. Tinley was just pulling herself together. "Here's probably all that's left of your husband's property," Blake said. "There's twenty-three thousand dollars in there."

Mrs. Tinley clapped a hand to her forehead. "Twenty-three thousand!" She sat down again.

"My advice is to take the money and go back home. Forget you ever knew J. J. Tinley."

"I'll never forget him," she said solemnly. "He was my husband."

Roberta said, "Mrs. Tinley, there's a stage leaving for Thermopolis at one-thirty."

"I can't leave until my husband is buried," she said.

"He's buried, ma'am, under a burned building."

"I must go up there to see his grave, at least!"

But Blake said firmly, "Ma'am, I don't think it would be good for the children. It's dinner time now. Why don't you feed your family and take the stage as Miss Blendick suggested?"

She looked at him. Her thoughts were hard to follow.

"This is a sad thing," Blake said, "but it may be sadder if you go up there. I think it quite proper that you should go back home this afternoon."

Mrs. Tinley left, with effusive thanks. Blake put his hat back on.

Roberta studied him. "Why were you so determined that she should not go up on Crazyman?"

"If Mrs. Tinley goes nosing around she'll find out about some things she doesn't need to know." He started hunting for makin's. "The worst of it is, I think she has a suspicion already."

"A suspicion of what?"

"Everything in general," he said evasively, and found a package of cigarette papers. "Well, I'm out lookin' for a place to 'light again. Reckon I'll be saying so long, Miss Roberta."

She came a little closer. He found a sack of Bull Durham and worked it open with his forefinger. "Do you really want to stay put?" she asked.

"I wanted to stay put years ago," he said, "down in Albany County."

"And you have to move now?"

"The Indians have got my water rights," he said. "The Land Office will cancel my filing and let me file somewhere else. I'd better go while I can." He made a trough of the cigarette paper with his left hand and began to shake tobacco into it.

"You've still got stock, haven't you?"

"Something over two hundred head."

"Where are you taking it?"

He caught the paper tag in his teeth and closed the bag. "Somewhere else," he said, and began to roll the cigarette out smooth and plump.

"There's a nice piece of land over on Gunsmoke Creek, just above my place," she said. "Some water too."

He licked the paper, smoothed it, twisted the ends, and put it in his mouth.

"There's no upper fence on my place," she added. "It's sort of a box canyon up there, and I never needed a fence."

He struck a match on the seat of his levis.

"I suppose I'd have to run a fence line between us, but —"

He looked at her over the match flame. Suddenly he tossed the match through the open door. He got rid of the cigarette with a "ptt!" and put his arms around her. "That won't be necessary, Miss Roberta," he said as the cigarette came to rest in a corner.

About the Author

Noel (Miller) Loomis was born in Oklahoma Territory and retained all his life a strong Southwestern heritage. One of his grandfathers made the California Gold Rush in 1849 and another was in the Cherokee Strip land rush in 1893. He grew up in Oklahoma, New Mexico, Texas, and Wyoming, areas in the American West that would figure prominently in his Western stories. His parents operated an itinerant printing and newspaper business and, as a boy, he learned to set lead type by hand. Although he began contributing Western fiction to the magazine market in the late 1930s, it was with publication of his first novel, RIM OF THE CAPROCK (1952), that he truly came to prominence. This novel is set in Texas, the location of two other notable literary endeavors, TEJAS COUNTRY (1953) and THE TWILIGHTERS (1955). These novels evoke the harsh, even savage violence of an untamed land in a graphic manner that eschewed sharply the romanticism of fiction so characteristic of an earlier period in the literary history of the Western story. In these novels, as well as WEST TO THE SUN (1955), SHORT CUT TO RED RIVER (1958), and CHEYENNE WAR CRY (1959), Loomis very precisely sets forth a precise time and place in frontier history and proceeds to capture the ambiance of the period in descriptions, in attitudes responding to the events of the day, and laconic dialogue that etches vivid characters set against these historical backgrounds. In the second edition of TWENTIETH CENTURY WESTERN WRITERS (1991), the observation is made that Loomis's work was "far ahead of its time. No other Western writer of the 1950s depicts so honestly the nature of the land and its people, and renders them so alive. Avoiding comment, he concentrates on the atmosphere of time and place. One experiences with him the smell of Indian camps and frontier trading posts, the breathtaking vision of the Caprock, the sudden terror of a surprise attack. Loomis, in his swift character sketches, his striking descriptions, his lithe effective style, brings that world to life before our eyes. In the field he chose, he has yet to be surpassed."

ISIS publish a wide range of books in large print, from fiction to biography. Any suggestions for books you would like to see in large print or audio are always welcome. Please send to the Editorial Department at:

ISIS Publishing Limited
7 Centremead
Osney Mead
Oxford OX2 0ES

A full list of titles is available free of charge from:

Ulverscroft Large Print Books Limited

(UK)
The Green
Bradgate Road, Anstey
Leicester LE7 7FU
Tel: (0116) 236 4325

(Australia)
P.O. Box 314
St Leonards
NSW 1590
Tel: (02) 9436 2622

(USA)
P.O. Box 1230
West Seneca
N.Y. 14224-1230
Tel: (716) 674 4270

(Canada)
P.O. Box 80038
Burlington
Ontario L7L 6B1
Tel: (905) 637 8734

(New Zealand)
P.O. Box 456
Feilding
Tel: (06) 323 6828

Details of **ISIS** complete and unabridged audio books are also available from these offices. Alternatively, contact your local library for details of their collection of **ISIS** large print and unabridged audio books.